The Curse of King Toot

The Curse of King Toot

John's Fart-Ripping Adventures Book 1

John Pahrsink

Derelict Books

To: Paul Hunn, of Flint, Michigan who allegedly let out a fart lasting a whopping two minutes and forty-two seconds.

While it may not be an official Guinness World Record, I salute you.

FOREWORD
A NOTE FROM THE AUTHOR

Before I begin telling my story, I should probably introduce myself. My name is John Pahrsink Jr, and I'm cursed to fart out ghosts for all eternity. I know you're laughing right now. Go ahead. I'll wait.

...

Yes. I'm aware that 'John' is slang for toilet. And also, since my dad's name is John, that makes me number two. Get it out. It doesn't bother me anymore. Thanks to my unique condition, I've heard all the potty-themed jokes.

...

Are you done laughing yet? Good. Because I can assure you there's nothing funny about my intestinal issue. But since I have your attention, I might as well explain how it all began.

Everything you're about to read is true. So, if you've got any bright ideas for a cure, feel free to interrupt at any time.

My story begins on the first day of the fifth grade.

CHAPTER 1
BUS-TED

The curtains flew open by a ghostly presence, blinding my barely open eyes with the morning sun. I groaned. It was worse than a ghost. It was Mom, frowning while she navigated the minefield of moving boxes covering my bedroom floor.

"Get up, sleepy head."

I pulled the comforter over my head. "Five more minutes, Mom."

"Nope." She ripped the entire blanket from my hands and tossed it off the bed. "You're going to school and then after you get home, you're cleaning up this mess."

We moved to the suburbs of Chicago almost a month ago for dad's new teaching job. I was the last one to unpack my stuff.

"Please?" I put on my best puppy-dog eyes. "I'm not feeling well. I probably shouldn't even go to school today."

Mom sat on the edge of the bed and pressed her clammy hand against my forehead.

"You feel fine to me."

"I don't have a fever," I said. "It's my stomach. I have a bad feeling about today..."

"Like Aunt Lucille."

Mom gave me the side-eye.

Her sister was the family kook, convinced she could see the future, spirits, and signs invisible to everyone else.

"Okay. If you feel that strongly, you can stay home."

My eyebrows flinched, but I kept the rest of the surprise off my face. I've tried this at least once a month. Was today really the day it worked?

"But..."

And there it was. Three simple letters guaranteed to destroy any kid's hope.

"You're going to clean this room."

I looked around. A pile of dirty clothes sat at the foot of the bed. The bookshelf sat empty in the corner. Boxes loaded with books, board games, and clothes outnumbered anything I'd actually put away.

It was a miracle Mom let me get away with it this long.

"Okay," I said. No big deal. I could have this done in a few hours and have the rest of the day to myself.

"And help me clean the bathrooms, dry the dishes, fold laundry—"

I bolted up. "Ya know what? I think I'm feeling better."

Mom held her palms up. "Look at that. It's a miracle."

"I still think it's stupid the first day of school is on a Thursday. The week's more than half over."

"Just get dressed and eat breakfast so you don't miss the bus. Unless you want to help clean—"

My butt was out of bed before the word "toilets" left her lips.

I scooped a pair of shorts from the floor, plunged one foot inside, and promptly lost my balance.

"Oof," I said, falling back into bed. "And what kind of school starts fifth grade with a field trip?"

Mom ignored the question and looked down her nose at me. "Are those clean?"

"Clean enough," I said with a shrug.

She shook her head. "At least put on new underwear."

With that, she closed the door and left me alone with my mess.

The closet squeaked as I threw the door open. Right... empty hangers and more moving boxes. So far, I've been taking what I needed straight from the boxes. In a few months, they'd unpack themselves.

Now I saw the problems with that plan. This was the first day of fifth grade we were talking about. My choice of clothes was the first thing everyone would see.

A licensed Minecraft or superhero shirt would lump me with the nerd crowd. I went through that at my last school. Don't get me wrong, I liked them. I just wished my circle of friends were larger.

I ripped the tape off the closest cardboard box. It contained all long-sleeved shirts, a death sentence in the ninety degrees of August in Chicago.

Unfortunately, I didn't know what to wear that would attract the cool kids. Or even which box held them.

"Are you dressed yet?" Mom yelled. "You're going to miss the bus."

I jerked my head up to respond and noticed a tiny hint of color peeking through the darkness providing hope. I tossed aside the dark shirts and found a solid, red tee shirt. Primary colors were safe, right? Once I fit in with a crowd, I'd tailor my wardrobe accordingly.

I slipped the shirt over my head and jogged down the stairs. Dad sat at the kitchen table in his work suit, leaning over a bowl of cereal while fiddling with his cellphone.

"Sackbut!" he exclaimed.

Mom appeared like a ninja, with that look on her face when any of us disappointed her. "John!"

"Not you, Honey. It's thirteen down. 'A Renaissance-era brass instrument similar to a trumpet.'"

I shook my head. Dad had a crazy obsession with words. Obscure word-of-the-day subscriptions, daily crossword puzzles, Scrabble, they were all his jam. In a roundabout way, that's why we moved out here from North Dakota. His mastery of the English language (and more) had earned him a job as Elmhurst University's newest linguistics professor.

Hmm... Do you know that word? Dad is a giant word nerd. He's fluent in four languages: English, French, Spanish, and Italian. I can barely manage English, but I DO have a larger vocabulary than most kids my age. I'll try to leave some notes in the margins if I use a big word.

Linguistics is the study of language and its structure. Now that you know that I'll let you get back to the story.

I threw open the cabinet door, which banged it into its neighbor. Crossword or not, it got Dad's attention.

"Good morning, John," he said as I pulled down the family-sized box of Lucky Charms.

When he didn't get a response, he repeated himself.

"I said good morning, John."

"It's the first day of school," I said with a groan as I shuffled to the other side of the kitchen and fished a bowl out of the cabinet. "What's so good about it?"

"Maybe if you ask nicely, they'll let you play the sackbut in music class."

Mom appeared in the kitchen again. "Stop saying that word." She took the cereal box from my hands. "And you, find something healthier for breakfast."

"But Dad's eating it!"

"Well, your father is a terrible role model."

"Hey, I resemble that remark." Dad made eye contact with me and smiled before whispering 'Sackbut' again.

Mom abandoned the cereal box on the counter and shook her finger. "I heard that. We don't need him repeating that."

It provided just enough distraction to fill my bowl with multi-colored marshmallows. As lame as his jokes were, Dad always had my back.

I hurried to the table before Mom could take away my breakfast.

"Thanks," I whispered.

He winked, grabbed the milk carton in front of him, and topped off my bowl.

"When I was your age, we didn't get field trips on the first day of school. You'll have fun. And you'll finally meet some kids your age."

Of course, they were right. School was the best place to meet kids. Our new neighborhood was full of retirees.

On the one hand, it was great. The sweet old lady with the wiener dog next door kept dropping off cookies. Though, unless I wanted to learn cribbage, it left me without playmates.

But being shy and the idea of talking to strangers— even if they were kids—terrified me.

Dad mumbled under his breath as he continued through his crossword, and I saw an opportunity.

I brought my elbow to my mouth and let out what I hoped was a convincing cough.

"Mom already told me you tried pull this on her," he said without looking up from his phone. "You're not fooling anyone."

I threw my head back. "Come on, Dad. You said it yourself—when you were my age, they didn't have field trips on the first day of school. That's suspicious. I mean, what do we *really* know about this place?"

"You're going."

"But Leyla—"

"Your sister doesn't start until next Tuesday. Next year, you'll get a few extra days off, too."

"But—"

"But nothing. You're going to school, and that's final."

"Fine," I grumbled, and ate my cereal in silence.

Mom came out of nowhere and whisked away both mine and Dad's empty bowls. "Oh. I didn't have a chance to pack your lunch. Good thing you're old enough to do it now."

The dishwasher door slammed shut with a dull thud. By the time I turned around, Mom was gone, further cementing my belief in her past life as a ninja.

I pushed in my chair and dug through the cabinets beneath the island countertop. There was only one option: an old Paw Patrol lunch box that tragically survived the move.

"Where are the rest of the lunch bags?"

"Somewhere among all the boxes in your room," Dad said without looking up.

Great. Simply great. Paper bags were cool, right?

When I stood up to get to the fridge, my big sister was in my way. Apparently, she was part ninja, too.

"Move. You're gonna make me late for school."

I regretted the words as soon as they left my mouth.

Leyla moved with all the speed of a sloth stuck in mud.

"Don't worry, I'm almost done."

I tried to squeeze in, but she stretched her body further, keeping me out. Leyla plucked a yogurt off the shelf. Her hand went into one of the drawers and closed around something before stepping out of my way.

I held up the sandwich container. The yellow stains on the side of the Tupperware signaled Mom put too much mustard in the egg salad again. With a sigh, I threw it in the bag.

At least we had fruit punch Capri Sun to wash it down. One of those went into the bag as well. I pulled open the left drawer but only found cold cuts and a pound of ground beef destined for whatever Mom planned for dinner. The right drawer held all kinds of cheeses: shredded, sliced, logs of goat cheese.

But something was missing. Those little cheese wheels covered in red wax.

My beloved Babybel.

I spun around and glared at my sister. "Give it back, twerp."

Leyla stood safely beside Dad's chair.

"I don't know what you're talking about."

"You took the last Babybel I was going to put in my lunch."

She uncurled her fingers, one by one, like a supervillain dangling their death ray key above the helpless hero. "I didn't see your name on it."

I dropped my lunch on the counter and lunged at her. Leyla held the miniature wheel of cheese above my head. She was too fast, not to mention a foot taller than me.

"That's mine!"

"Nope. I got here first, four-eyes."

"Dad..."

"Sorry, John, but it's nacho cheese," Dad said.

Both Leyla and I groaned. If there was one thing we always agreed on, it was that Dad needed to lay off the dad jokes.

"Can't you pick something else?"

"But she doesn't even like Babybel cheese!"

"Yeah, I do."

"Really? I've never seen you eat one."

"Fine," Leyla said as she tore the cellophane open with her claws. She peeled apart the protective wax, stepped on the garbage can lever, and then dropped everything inside.

"It slipped." She grabbed the sides of the bin and looked inside. It was convincing, but I knew she did it on purpose. "Honest."

My face grew warm. Before I could do anything that I regretted, Dad stepped between us.

"We'll get more cheese, John. I'm off to chiro and then work." Dad messed up my hair as he stepped away. "That's the chiropractor, not Cairo, Egypt," he called behind him.

Mom appeared in the kitchen again. "Your shoes should be on and marching your butt out the door by now."

"I'm still packing. Leyla stole the last Babybel."

She took the brown paper bag from my hands. "I'll find you something else. Go pack your school bag."

"Pack it with what? You ordered all my supplies ahead of time. All I need for the field trip is my lunch."

"Except for something to entertain you during the hour-long bus ride."

My stomach dropped. Hour-long bus ride.

I ran around the house like crazy, searching in cabinets, in closets, under couches. "Where are all my sketch pads?"

My sister followed me from room to room, snickering. "I know where they are."

"Please, Leyla," I said, grabbing her by the shoulders and looking up into her brown eyes. "Help me."

"They're in all those cardboard boxes in your room."

I swear the next words she said came out in Mom's voice.

"You should have unpacked."

This time I saw Mom coming. She shoved my backpack into my hands, grabbed my bicep, and led me to the front door.

"But I don't have anything for the bus."

"Then you'd better hope your seatmate will share because if you miss the bus, you're cleaning toilets."

With that, Mom pushed me onto the front porch. I had enough time to turn around and look down at my socks before my sneakers hit me in the chest.

"Have a good day at school, and don't forget to zip up your backpack," she said, closing the door behind her.

I laced up my shoes, hiked the bag on my shoulder, and headed down the driveway.

"*You're* cleaning the toilets," I mumbled as I kicked an acorn across the sidewalk. My shoelace caught under my other foot and pulled loose.

With a sigh, I bent down and redid the loop. As I stood, a school bus turned onto the street a block ahead of me. A kid in the back window pointed and laughed as they rumbled down the street.

CHAPTER 2
YOU CAN PICK YOUR FRIENDS

I was too young to clean toilets. Bleach? Harmful chemicals? There had to be a law against anyone under eighteen from using those.

The bus sped off without so much as slowing. I guess living in a neighborhood full of retirees meant the bus stop was a ghost town.

Several options presented themselves in my head as I shuffled back home. One, I hurry home and apologize. If I moved quickly enough, Mom could follow the bus to the next stop.

Two, I stalled, ensuring that I missed not only the bus to school, but also the bus to the museum. Mom wouldn't drive into the city. It might land me on toilet duty, but how long did cleaning a toilet take? Surely, there'd be time for video games. If Mom didn't ground me.

I stopped on the sidewalk square in front of our house. Of course, there was a third choice. I sneak back into the house and up to the game room, making sure I kept the TV volume on low. I could pull off a six-hour video game marathon session without blinking.

You know full well what I chose. And I was sure I'd pull it off. My lunch bag and water bottle were still in my bag. If I had to pee, I'd go right out the window. No need to alarm Mom with the sound of a flushing toilet. I even nestled my shoes into my backpack so they wouldn't squeak on the tile floor.

I depressed the little button on the door. Mom locked it behind her. No big deal. We had one of those digital locks, and the password was the same as our old house. I paused after each keypress to ensure the rapid beeping wouldn't attract attention.

The mechanical lock whirred the sweet sound of success, and I was one step closer. I'd be upstairs in less than a minute and nobody would be the wiser. I held my breath and pushed the door open.

A chime rang deep within the house.

I sucked in my lips and snapped my eyes shut. Oh yeah... the security system.

"What are you doing back so—" Mom stepped into the hallway and did a double take. "You missed the bus."

"I missed the bus."

Her head panned down. "And where are your shoes?"

"It wasn't my fault. I barely made it off the porch before the bus sped past," I stammered. "Yeah... the bus driver was a maniac. He flew right through the stop sign."

She looked at me skeptically. "I'll grab my keys and drive you to school. Get your shoes on."

Images of poo-stained toilets prevented any arguing on my part.

My shoes went on in record time and I hopped into the back seat of Mom's car before she changed her mind.

We drove in silence through our new neighborhood and past the middle school I'd attend next year.

"You won't have to worry about missing the bus next year since you'll walk with your sister."

"Uh huh," I mumbled.

She said something else, but I couldn't tell you what. I was too busy running through all the terrible outcomes of the upcoming school year. Not to mention having Mom drop me off on the first day of school.

She believed in tough-love parenting. I let her down twice today. In her eyes, missing the bus was a direct result of me never cleaning my room. Mom would ensure I learned a lesson. Probably by embarrassing the snot out of me.

I swallowed and thought of the last time I missed the bus. Mom had honked the horn when she'd dropped me off. While everyone looked, she'd jumped out of the car and planted a loud, overexaggerated smooch on my forehead.

Maybe I deserved that one a teensy bit. I'd snuck off and played video games while she sat on a conference call and missed the alarm. Still, kids had mocked me for months.

"I'm sorry, Mom," I said, gripping the backpack in my lap. "When I get home, I'll clean my room. I swear. This won't happen tomorrow."

She glanced my way and sighed. "You're just lucky I have this week off work."

The car slowed to a stop behind a single school bus, and Mom threw the car into park.

My breath caught in my chest. I felt it coming. Social pariah, part two. *An outcast or reject*

Mom patted my leg. "I know this move hasn't been easy. I packed a surprise with your lunch. Have a good first day, honey."

"Thanks, Mom."

I held my breath, but there was no horn-honking, no kisses, no shouting a cutesy nickname. I grabbed the top handle of my bag and never looked back.

The lone adult standing in the grass, a woman in a long scarlet dress, walked toward me. With a large head full of curly black hair and a pair of glasses thicker than my pinky, she definitely looked like a teacher.

"Are you the new fifth grade student?" She looked down at the clipboard in her hand. "John Pahrsink?"

"Yeah. That's me."

She made a little check mark and waved toward the bus. "You're the last to arrive. We'll welcome you to fifth grade tomorrow. For now, we've got a schedule to keep."

"Sorry," I said, following the woman. "The bus didn't wait for me."

The accordion doors closed behind us and the driver peered down at me. He was old enough to be my grandfather (and possessed a similar bald spot and large belly).

"Hurry up and find a seat."

Heh. He sounded like my grandpa's, too.

I started down the aisle and swallowed.

Everyone on the bus stared at the new kid who'd held up their departure. My eyes scanned the rows of seats as I wandered forward. Adults sat by themselves in the first two seats on either side.

Sitting with the chaperones was a bad idea. I did NOT want to become the teacher's pet.

A tall girl with braces was my next option. I paused ever so slightly and pushed the glasses up on my nose. She moved her backpack from the floor onto the seat, and I kept going.

My eyes drifted over dozens of my peers as I marched down the aisle. The kids here looked no different from those at my old school in Iowa.

However, I knew that picking a spot on the bus was a major decision. It would be my first opportunity to side with one of the cliques.———→ Group of people with shared interests

There was an open spot next to a kid in a football jersey. A girl who must have been his twin sat on the other side of the aisle. Nope. Too jocky. Nobody in my family followed sports, so we'd have nothing in common.

Close to them was some weirdo in a fishing jacket. I didn't need *that*.

"Just pick a seat," someone in the back moaned.

I moved faster.

After shuffling back another ten feet I realized there were no more open seats.

I spun on my heels. It was either the fisherman or one of the jocks. My butt slammed onto the poorly padded seat before I realized what hit me.

"Sit down, new guy," the freckled kid beside me said, letting go of my bag.

Somehow, I missed an empty seat right in front of me. He was almost twice as big as me and built like a football player. What little hair remained on the top of the kid's buzz cut had been dyed green.

I couldn't believe it. The cool crowd found me.

The bus started rolling and he stuck out his hand.

"I'm Joe," the kid said. He pulled his hand away before I could even shake it. "Joe Mama!"

He laughed for a moment, then got serious again.

"I'm Stephen. With a P.H. What's your story?"

This was it. The most popular kid in school sat beside me. The rest of my social life depended upon how I answered. Only I didn't know *how* to answer. I set my backpack on the floor, stalling for time.

"Uhh…"

Stick to the facts, John, I thought. And then I realized something. I didn't *have* to be John. I could be someone cooler.

"I'm J.P. I just moved from Iowa."

Stephen's nose scrunched up. "Iowa?"

Telling someone you used to live in Iowa isn't impressive. Noted.

I switched tactics.

"Yeah. It sucked. But at least our school year didn't start with a stupid field trip on a Thursday."

He chuckled. For a second, I thought I was golden. Only his laughter didn't let up.

"It's not the first day of school," he said between more laughter.

"What do you mean?"

"This field trip was optional. Your mom wanted you out of her hair a day early."

"What?"

I lowered my head. *Would Mom really do that?*

Who am I kidding? Of course, she would. That's why she didn't get mad about me missing the bus. She felt guilty.

"It's okay. My mom did the same. We'll just have to make them regret it."

Looking back, that was a red flag (and the stupid Joe Mama thing was another). But I missed them due to a combination of sheer nervousness and all the gravestones flying past the bus window.

I pulled my feet off the floor and held my breath.

Stephen turned and watched me.

"What the heck are you doing?"

He followed my gaze as I pointed outside.

"What?"

I took a gasping breath as the last gravestone left our view.

"It's something my dad taught me. Ghosts can possess you if you don't hold your breath while passing a cemetery."

"There's no such thing as ghosts, dummy."

I knew that, but it was a family tradition.

As I put my foot down, it caught on my backpack and knocked the bag over. A glint of light reflecting off something apparently provided distraction from my silly superstition.

"You snuck in a gaming console?"

"What?" I said, looking down. "No."

But it was too late. His giant mitts yanked my bag open. A zipper tooth flew up and bounced off my glasses.

"Wait, what the heck is this thing?" Stephen asked, holding up the sleek black device.

I'd forgotten I had the pocket translator Dad gave me after his business trip to Spain last year. Apparently, I shoved it in the bag before the move. It probably wasn't cool, but I had an idea to win him over.

"It's something my dad gave me." I snatched the device back. "Here..."

I typed "butt" into the little keyboard and hit enter.

"Trasero," the robotic feminine voice announced.

I looked over at my seatmate. He didn't seem particularly impressed.

"That's 'butt' in Spanish."

Stephen stared at me, and I thought I'd break into a sweat. Then he smiled as he figured the device out. "Wait. Can you make it swear in any language?"

"Yeah, pretty much," I said with a shrug.

"Let me try." He pried the thing from my hand again.

His pudgy fingers fumbled with the keys. A minute later, we were both treated to the fruits of his labor.

"Beso mi trasero."

I leaned around the seat. The bus was loud enough that none of the teachers heard. Unless he dialed up the volume to eleven.

"*BESO MI TRASERO!*" screamed the pocket translator.

The curly-haired teacher who'd guided me onto the bus popped into the aisle.

Cool. My new friend just told the entire bus to kiss his butt.

CHAPTER 3
YOU CAN'T PICK YOUR FRIEND'S NOSE

My hand flailed around blindly, searching for the pocket translator, while my eyes remained locked on the teacher. The device was mine. Which meant I'd take the blame.

I didn't know whether you could get detention before the first day of school. Either way, I was getting grounded.

That soulless, robotic voice spoke up again. Before it could give away our position, my fingers finally found the little power button.

Only the gift from my dad was warmer and wetter than I recalled.

I glanced over. Nope. Not the translator. My pointer finger was knuckle deep in Stephen's nose.

A sharp pain burned through my shoulder as his fist connected.

On the plus side, the electronic swear machine slipped from his hand and hit the ground. The battery compartment popped open and one of the double A's rolled to the back of the bus.

"Sorry," I said, rubbing my throbbing shoulder. "That teacher was on her way back here."

Stephen rose until he could see over the seat tops. "Mrs. Barwick," he growled. "That old witch never returned the comics she took from me last year."

I leaned down and stuffed the device at the bottom of my bag.

By the time I looked up, Mrs. Barwick hovered directly above me.

"Something the matter, John?"

"No." I held up the bag of chips that had fallen out of my lunch sack. "Just knocked over my bag."

"I see." She eyed my Fritos and steadied herself with the seat as the bus nailed a pothole. The battery let out a clunk as it hit one of the walls in the back.

"Just remember, no eating on the bus. Or inside the museum."

"Then how will we have lunch?" Stephen asked.

Mrs. Barwick's eyes narrowed into murderous slits I'd never seen before on a teacher. "No eating outside the designated lunch areas."

"Oh," he said, nodding. "Right."

I stared at the seatback and swallowed a lump in my throat. Talking back to teachers was another red flag. I'd befriended a madman.

She started toward her seat and addressed the rest of the bus. "We'll be at the museum in a few minutes. Make sure you have all your belongings. While we'll have the same bus on our return trip, we won't have access until the end of the day."

I looked behind me. There was no point going back for the battery. It was safest in its new home, keeping both mine and Stephen's "trasero" out of trouble.

I pulled my bag into my lap and tugged on the zipper. Naturally, it refused to budge. I gave it a good yank only for the pull to come off in my hand.

Just great, I thought with a sigh. I pulled the other end as close to the broken tooth as possible and swung the bag onto my back.

"Watch it," Stephen said, pushing the bag out of his face. There was another faint rip of the zipper weakening.

We filed out of the bus and onto the sidewalk in front of the Field Museum. The large white, columned building was reminiscent of the Museum of Natural History on the University of Iowa campus. Except, of course, that it was at least three times larger.

Mrs. Barwick took charge again and stepped in front of the growing mass of children.

"Please pair into groups of two or three to ensure nobody gets lost. Make sure you give the tour guides the same respect you'd show me."

She took that moment to affix her gaze on Stephen and me.

"This is a school-sanctioned event, which means you can earn yourself detention by disobeying the museum's rules."

Great... It's not even the first day of school and the teacher's already watching me like a hawk.

My future classmates split into a dozen directions, leaving Stephen and me alone in the center of a wide circle. He grabbed my arm and pulled me closer.

"You're with me, new guy."

I know what you're thinking. Nobody else wanted to be in a group with "the most popular kid in school." How many red flags was that by now? I'd lost count, and that's something I'll regret for the rest of my life.

My legs ached as we trudged up the dozens of shallow steps. What awaited inside the main doors was worth it. A thirty-foot-long dinosaur skeleton loomed over us in the middle of the three-story-tall foyer. At the far end of the room was another. That one I recognized by the sail-shaped bony plates on its back. Spinosaurus.

I looked up as I walked closer to the first dinosaur. Soaring above us was another larger-than-life skeleton. A Pterosaur.

The overstimulated nerd side of my brain was too excited to reel in. "Could you imagine when these things roamed the earth?"

Stephen was silent for a moment, and I thought I'd made a mistake. What kind of kid doesn't like dinosaurs?

"Yeah. Too bad they're gone. We could get this guy to eat Mrs. Barwick."

"Look at its teeth," I said, looking down at the little plaque. "The Titanosaur only ate plants."

He rolled his eyes. "Whatever. Then it could squash her."

I let the excitement fade from my face. Stephen wasn't excited to be here. If I wanted to fit in, I shouldn't be, either.

Someone cleared their throat, and I turned away from the dinos. A balding man with a short grey beard waved his arm in the air. The bright blue shirt with the word 'Volunteer' on it was a dead giveaway as to who he was.

"My name is Mr. Wyatt, and I'll be your guide for the day. If you have any questions along the way, please don't hesitate to raise your hands."

He rose on his tiptoes and looked across the group. "None so far? Good. We're going to start with the Native Truths exhibit."

Our group steered away from the skeletal behemoths through an opening into the next section. Glass display cases lined the walls holding beaded shirts, wooden flutes, rugs, and other artifacts.

"Prior to Europe's colonization of the Americas, the land beneath our feet belonged to The Council of the Three Fires. This was comprised of individuals from the Ojibwe, Odawa, Potawatomi, and many additional smaller nations.

"That is, until their relocation to reservations. Here you will find their stories preserved via written word, song, dance, and art.

"Feel free to wander around the room and inspect these artifacts."

The jersey-wearing twins ran in front of us to a large touchscreen monitor. As they swiped their fingers across the display, flutes, drums, and vocals mingled together. I walked in their direction to wait for a turn.

"This is boring," Stephen proclaimed. "It's just dumb clothes and stuff."

He headed in the opposite direction toward a bench and then paused. "You comin', J.P?"

Hearing Stephen call me by the cool new nickname I totally just made up was too much to turn down.

"Yeah."

We spent the next fifteen minutes on that bench in relative silence. Stephen picked his nose and wiped the leftovers on the carpeted floor. Every so often I picked up laughter and music coming from the mini recording studio.

I gazed longingly at the other fifth graders bouncing from case to case, cracking jokes, and generally enjoying themselves.

My eyes fell on an especially long booger my new friend had left dangerously close to my sneaker.

I'd picked the wrong partner. Only I hadn't picked him. Maybe it was my imagination, but my shoulder throbbed from when he'd hit me earlier. Stephen didn't seem like a kid who handled rejection well. I was stuck with him for the rest of the day.

At least.

"Riverview Elementary students, please line up," came Mrs. Barwick's voice.

Stephen didn't budge. Luckily, since we were in the middle of the room, nobody noticed our noncompliance.

The museum tour guide appeared again. "From here, we will enter the Pawnee Earth Lodge."

We joined the line at the tail end of the group and moved into another room. A room with an entire building inside it. Well, less of a building and more of a primitive dome structure made of timber beams, twigs, straw, and mud.

Animal furs and woven blankets lined the walls and lay atop wooden cots. Split logs rested in a teepee-like configuration within the center of the home.

I stepped near the middle of the structure and looked up. Pinpoints of light shone down on us like the night sky.

Certain the entire group had arrived, the man began his well-rehearsed spiel. ——→ *A long speech*

"Welcome to the museum's earth lodge. You're standing in a replica home Native American people would have lived in during the eighteen hundreds.

"Members of the Pawnee nation assisted during the creation of the structure you see here. After its creation, holy men blessed the sacred space at the back of the lodge."

He gestured to a small, roped-off area opposite the entrance.

"You are welcome to lie down on the beds and examine any replica tools within this space. Out of respect to the native peoples, we ask that you not disturb the blessed space.

"Are there any questions?"

"How many people lived in here?" someone asked.

"Good question. Several families would have shared this space, as well as the household duties. Something unique about the Indigenous culture is that it was a matriarchal society.

"Does anyone know what that means?"

I spoke up without thinking. "It means the women were in charge."

He nodded at me and smiled. "That's right. Women were the prime decision makers. When a couple married, the man moved in with his new wife's family."

All the adults laughed as one of the male teachers mumbled, "No thank you."

Kids tested out the beds, exclaiming how hard they were. Others ran their fingers or brushed their cheeks against the soft animal hides. Stephen had his eyes set on one thing only.

"What do you think is in the basket back there?" he asked, nodding toward the one place we weren't allowed.

I knew where this was headed and tried to dissuade him. "Maybe poisonous herbs."

"Nah. Not if they let school kids in here. I'm going to find out."

"You can't."

I watched as Stephen turned around and his fingers balled up again like on the bus. That phantom pain returned, making me rethink my approach.

"There are too many teachers. They'll catch you."

"No, they're not even paying attention."

I glanced back and realized he was right. Our chaperones were too busy asking their own questions and chit-chatting with the tour guide or each other.

Stephen's pointer finger jabbed me in the chest. "Besides, you're gonna keep watch."

A lump grew in my throat as he started ducking beneath the rope. This was decidedly worse than making my translator swear in Spanish. I couldn't exactly stop him by sticking my finger in his nose again.

I raised my fist to my mouth and coughed into my hand.

The guide stopped mid-sentence and looked over at us. Along with every. Single. Teacher.

Stephen bolted up straight.

Mrs. Barwick crossed her arms, marched across the lodge, and stood guard beside the off-limits area.

My museum partner's eyes narrowed to tiny slits.

I closed my eyes and waited for the pummeling.

"What the heck did you do that for?" Stephen whispered.

I stepped closer to the rest of the class, out of our chaperone's earshot. "That was me watching your back. She saw you and was already headed your way."

He stared right through the lie and into my eyes. "Right... And what was that with the 'matry—thingie'? I'm starting to think you're not cool at all."

The group flowed out of the earth lodge, through the darkened corridor, and into the next gallery. I quickened my steps. If I could stick near one of the teachers, maybe I'd escape without a museum-worthy collection of bruises.

Stephen grabbed the top of my bag and held me back. *Riiip.*

I twisted around. My fingers found the distinct texture of a brown paper bag. The tear in my zipper was at least twice as big.

"Oops," was all my partner said before walking off.

This room had totem poles stretching all the way to the ceiling. I thought they were cool, but the rest of the class crowded around the glass cases opposite them. Those displays held painted masks with menacing faces, giant noses, and animalistic features of all sorts.

I'd like to tell you that I joined them. That I made new friends while checking out those cool masks. And that together, we stood up to Stephen.

Instead, I opted to save what little life my backpack had left and stuck by his side near the enormous totem platform.

"You've got one last chance to prove yourself," Stephen said, his eyes locked on the elaborately carved tree trunk in front of us. "Hit the bear between the eyes."

"What?"

Stephen snorted and hacked and chewed before tilting his head back and spitting into the air.

There were six teachers and a tour guide somewhere behind us and he didn't even look. At that point, I was afraid to turn around.

My eyes locked on the wad of phlegm that smacked into the eagle's beak.

He laughed and elbowed my side.

"Come on. Your turn."

I took a deep breath and looked over the statue.

A brown creature with large front teeth, probably a beaver, formed the base. On its shoulders sat the larger bear. Above it was something green. A frog, maybe?

At the very top was the eagle. The regal bird had its wings outstretched, as if desperately reaching for a hankie.

Even if I'd wanted to spit onto the beautiful totem pole—and to be clear, I didn't (**AND NOBODY SHOULD**)—I couldn't. The salivary glands in my mouth went on strike and had nothing to give.

Stephen leaned so close I could smell the stink of his breath. "If you don't, I'll tell everyone you're the one who spit on the eagle."

I coughed and tried to work up whatever saliva I could.

Someone behind me cleared their throat. I spun around and gasped, spit dribbling down my chin. Mrs. Barwick grabbed both my and Stephen's shirt sleeves.

CHAPTER 4
HAVE A NICE TRIP, SEE YOU NEXT FALL

My heart beat furiously. My partner had just defiled a priceless cultural artifact and already had a plan for me to take the fall.

"The rest of the class moved ahead to the ancient Egypt wing. You're paired together so nobody gets lost. That only works if one of you pays attention."

I kept waiting for her to notice the giant loogie hanging from the eagle's beak, but somehow, she never looked up.

"Do I need to split the two of you up?"

"No, Mrs. Barwick," Stephen said before I had a chance to swallow the mouthful of spit.

She guided us back to the main lobby before letting go of our shirts. I looked over my shoulder, all too happy to escape the spit-covered totem.

"Sorry," our teacher said as we passed through a narrow entryway of another independent structure built inside the museum. Giant sand-colored bricks sat atop one another, like a pyramid if it were smaller and flat on top.

"No worries. We're just getting back to it." The guide smiled and gestured around the small room we'd packed into. "Welcome to ancient Egypt.

"This is the museum's 'mastaba,' a type of tomb used in Egypt. And the little pictures you see engraved into the wall are a picture-based language used by the Egyptian people known as hieroglyphics."

I touched the plexiglass-lined walls. Neat rows of birds, hands, eyes, and other symbols stretched across the entire room.

"Why is there plastic covering the walls?" a student asked. "Was this an actual tomb?"

"No," the guide explained. "But it's there to protect the stone from wear nonetheless."

Stephen grabbed my arm and pulled me atop a section of plexiglass set in the floor. I had enough time to look down through the shaft reaching to the floor below before he started jumping.

He laughed as I hurried off.

The guide cleared his throat and motioned us forward. "Follow me down the spiral staircase deeper into the mastaba. The rooms below our feet contain one of the largest mummy collections in the US."

There were several gasps from the crowd.

"Mummies are cursed," someone muttered.

Several other kids said something to similar effect.

"I don't want to see the mummies," a girl said.

"Quiet down, children," said the short male teacher in a white shirt and bowtie whose name I'd never learned. "Everybody will be fine."

The museum guide stepped in, his hands making calming gestures. "Okay, okay. How about I explain the curse of the mummy before we go downstairs."

All of us either nodded or responded in the affirmative.

I leaned closer as he spoke. From the corner of my eye, I noticed Stephen listening intently.

"There is some historical accuracy to the idea of 'The Mummy's Curse.' Many individuals have gotten sick, or even died following the opening of Tutankhamun's and other's tombs.

"However, the scientific community believes they're a result of toxic fungal spores. You have nothing to worry about because all the artifacts in the museum's possession went through a meticulous cleaning process. Furthermore, from an archeological standpoint, no recorded translations of hieroglyphics have ever mentioned specific curses.

"Now... who wants to see a mummified cat?"

Most of the boys' hands shot up in the air.

"Please hold onto the handrail on your way down and watch your step," he said as kids pushed toward the spiral staircase.

The air in the basement was noticeably cooler. Or maybe it was the thin ice I skated on with the only friend I'd made so far.

Cases filled with artifacts lined every wall. Our guide gestured to the one closest to the entrance. Jars, vases, and cups of all sizes lined the series of shelves within.

"Welcome inside the tomb. Within this storeroom you'll see everything the individual's spirit required to live comfortably in the afterlife.

"These alabaster and pottery bowls are only a small example of the belongings typically buried with their owner. You also would have found furniture, games, and hunting implements."

"Even food?" someone in front asked.

"Yes, even food. Typically in sealed jars, like these," he said, gesturing behind him. "They'd also be filled with beer and wine."

The guide resumed after another colorful comment by a teacher I didn't quite catch.

"Non-stoneware items either rotted over time or found their way into the possession of graverobbers."

Stephen rolled his eyes. "You said there were mummies down here."

"Yes. The first is in the very next chamber."

My partner rubbed his hands together and pushed his way through our classmates.

His voice echoed off the stone brick walls.

"What the heck?" (Only, I remember him saying something other than 'heck.')

For everything the next room held, mummies were not one of them. In their place stood a line of dark, stone statues. A framed X-ray rested against one in the center.

Our guide quickly followed.

"That ain't no mummy," Stephen said.

"The mummy is *inside* the sarcophagus. The fabric used in the bindings is old and fragile. Light, dust, humidity, and—"

"So, there's no mummies here. You could have just said that."

The man stared at Stephen and seemed to realize there was no getting through to him.

"Any other questions?" he asked, turning to face the rest of the group.

"What's that?" a nameless child asked. I followed the tip of their finger to a little machine mounted on the wall.

He smiled. "A seismic sensor. There is an active fault line in southern Illinois that can create quakes this far north. That device helps protect the contents of the museum."

We wandered around the sealed sarcophagi for a while, then moved onto the next area. This room was larger but held more of what we'd already seen. Large glass displays contained artifacts, each with their own stories written on a nearby sign.

One such was an urn the size of a football, lit by a golden shaft of light descending from the heavens.

(Probably a slight exaggeration, but that's how I remembered it.)

My classmates spread out and examined the various cases. The jar that seemed boring to everyone else seemed to call out to me.

"A canopic jar," I said to myself more than to anyone else as I walked up to the pedestal.

"If they were canopic jars, they'd be decorated with the busts of Egyptian gods. But it doesn't make this one any less valuable." The museum guide tapped the sign. "This was an offering to Unis-ankh, the individual who called this tomb home. Scans suggest it's filled with sealed canisters, perhaps containing cheese or honey.

He jerked his head to the side and hurried across the room. "Please, no touching the displays."

"It's a canopic jar..." Stephen's mocking voice said in my ear. "Psh. I knew you smelled like a loser."

He hip-checked me, setting off a chain reaction that changed my entire life. My lunch and the electronic translator fell from my unsecured backpack. But that was the least of my problems.

My back slammed into the display. The somehow unsecured cube of glass slid over several inches and struck the next domino in sequence: one irreplaceable, several-thousand-year-old vase.

Time passed at a snail's pace and the urn toppled as if it weighed no more than a feather. At first, I thought the ancient gods smiled down on me, blessing me with the time to stop it.

But it wasn't meant to be. My feet refused to move. Instead, images flashed through my head as the ancient clayware pot inched to its doom. These weren't flashbacks people claim to see during near death experiences. No. They were scenes that hadn't happened yet.

All the unreleased video games I'd been waiting for. My first kiss (blech). Learning to drive and my first car. Leyla leaving for college and having the house all to myself.

None of them would ever pass.

I'm so dead.

CHAPTER 5
NACHO CHEESE

The vase slammed against the pedestal. My eyes went wide as the seal broke and the stopper rolled out of the enclosure and onto the floor. I shut my eyes, which sent my other senses into overdrive.

Somewhere in the museum, a baby screamed.

Musty dust from ages past tickled my nostrils.

Heavy footfalls rushed in my direction. A clammy hand grabbed my wrist and yanked me to my feet. Even better. Deadly spores AND detention.

The voice that followed wasn't Mrs. Barwick's. Or another teacher's.

"Are you okay?"

I finally found the courage to open my eyes. It was the weird kid with the fishing jacket. He looked my age (duh. These were my future classmates) and had a pair of glasses just like mine.

"Yeah," I said, wiping my hands on my pants, hopefully removing any poisonous spores that hadn't infiltrated my nose. "Thanks."

Behind me, the twins in basketball jerseys went to work.

The boy scooped up the runaway orange and reunited it with my sandwich. Meanwhile, his sister righted the vase and slid the "protective" glass back into alignment.

Someone cleared their throat, and I found Mrs. Barwick looming over us. I had no idea whether she had any children, but she sure possessed that motherly intuition when trouble was afoot.

"Is there a problem, Mr. Pahrsink?"

She looked at each of us in turn, while the girl nudged the seal behind the pedestal with her shoe.

"He tripped," the girl twin said.

"And we helped him up," her brother added, dropping my lunch bag into my backpack.

Our teacher searched our faces once more, somehow missing the guilt literally dripping off my brow. Maybe the fact that the others were all smiles and cool as cucumbers helped.

"Keep up with the group, please."

She walked away completely oblivious to what had just happened.

Phew.

"You guys really saved my butt. Thanks."

That's when I should have joined their group. Instead, I rejoined Stephen's side. I must not have been thinking clearly thanks to the evil vase dust.

"What was inside the urn?" he asked.

"That's what you want to know?" My fingers clenched into a fist. Then I remembered he was twice the size of me. "A whole lot of dust that's probably cursed."

Stephen shrugged. "Nah. You heard the old guy. Everything in here is clean."

"Clean or not, you almost destroyed a priceless artifact."

"That's the museum's fault for having a broken display." He looked back at the vase as we kept walking. "It's got to be worth a fortune. Think anyone would notice if I stuck it in my backpack?"

I coughed up more dust, and the thought of convincing him to steal it crossed my mind. He'd caused enough trouble for me, and we'd only been friends for a few hours. What would happen over the course of the school year?

Before I had a chance, the teachers herded us from the exhibit. One of them raised his arms and addressed us.

"We'll have thirty minutes for lunch before continuing our tour. The restrooms are to the left. If you do require the restroom, please use the buddy system."

I turned to Stephen. "I need to go to the bathroom."

He kept walking toward the picnic tables. "I'm gonna eat first."

You know how when you *can't* do something, that's *all* you want to do? That's how my bladder felt.

Who needed the buddy system? We'd been wandering around the museum for hours; statistically I wouldn't be alone.

Or not. Apparently, all my classmates had supersized bladders because the men's bathroom was pitch dark.

"Hello?" I called, stepping inside.

The lights flickered to life, and a growl echoed back.

The hair on the back of my neck stood at attention. My gut screamed at me to run. But my bladder had other ideas. Walking around with a giant wet spot simply wasn't an option.

I took baby steps toward the line of urinals and angled my neck to look beneath the stall doors. Nothing but scuffed floor tiles.

I shook my head. Public bathrooms were scary, but it's not like there was a monster in there. I sauntered up to the first urinal and started doing my business.

The lights flickered off and then on again.

Another growl echoed through the room.

A scream escaped my lips, and I jumped. As my hand fumbled for my zipper, Stephen cackled from the bathroom entrance.

"I told you there's no curse."

I bolted toward him and slapped him across the face with my pee-covered hand.

Okay, I didn't... But that would have been really cool. Instead, I washed my hands three or four times while he walked away laughing.

I wiped my hands on a paper towel and stared into the mirror. It could have been worse. Both my shirt and my pants were dry. Stephen could have dragged me into a stall, tossed my lunch in the toilet, and given me a swirly.

When I stepped into the lunch area a few minutes later, I found

Stephen sharing a table with a small group of kids. And by sharing, I mean he was at one end, and they were at the other.

As soon as my bag hit the bench, Stephen picked up his things and walked across the room. He shoved his way into an already full bench. Kids slid over like dominos until one fell onto the floor.

The other kids at the table gave him some space, some of them relocating entirely. My former partner didn't look back.

"Scoot over," someone said. "Join us."

The weird kid with the fisherman's vest who had helped me up motioned me over. I looked at Stephen and back to them. Something told me they weren't the 'popular' kids. But they were already better friends than the alternative.

I slid down the bench.

"I'm John," said the fisherman. He gestured across the table. "And this is Akira and Park."

"Hi," the twins said together, leaving me clueless as to which was which.

"I'm John too... John Pahrsink. My dad calls me J.J. for John Junior. He's a John too."

"Seriously?" Other John said. "I'm a junior too. Technically, I'm the fifth in a long line of Johns."

"This is going to get confusing." The girl twin sighed. "How about we call him *Other John*?"

"I want to be Other John. He should be..." Other John shrugged. "Maybe we should call him New Guy."

"If you're Other John now, why do we have to give him a different name?" asked Akira. *Or was he Park?*

I smiled, still thoroughly confused. "I'm okay with whatever."

"Then it's settled," Other John said. "You're John. Now, before you officially join our circle, you have to pass a test."

"Okay," I said, nodding. "But I'm not spitting on any artifacts."

They all stared at me.

"Okay..." Other John said, raising an eyebrow. "Whatever. First question. Do you like Minecraft?"

I nodded.

"Pokémon?" one of the twins asked. I still didn't know which was which.

"Xbox?"

The three of them fired off one thing after another until I feared my head would roll off my shoulders.

"Sports?"

I shrugged to that one. "Not really."

"Well then, you can hang with us any time. I'm not sure why you teamed up with Stephen anyway."

"He didn't give me much of a choice."

"Seems about right," said the girl twin.

"He's a giant jerk," her brother added.

"Sorry," I said. "Which one are you again?"

The girl raised her hand. "I'm Akira. It means 'sunlight' in Thai."

"And that makes me Park."

Akira elbowed her brother. "Tell him."

He shook his head. "No."

"Tell me what?"

"Everyone does their best to steer clear of Butt-crack Steve," Park said.

"Huh?"

I directed my gaze to where he gestured with his head.

Sure enough, Stephen's pants rode a little too low for comfort.

"No," Akira said. "Tell him what *your* name means."

Park lowered his head and mumbled something I couldn't make out.

Other John snickered, and Park groaned.

Akira smiled. "It means 'gourd' in Korean."

"Gourd?"

"Yup. Like the bumpy Halloween decorations."

I looked between the two twins. "Wait. Are you Thai or Korean?"

"Both," they said together.

"Thai on Mom's side," Akira said.

"And Korean on Dad's," finished her brother.

Mrs. Barwick stood up from the table of teachers and waved her arms. "Just a reminder, our tour resumes in fifteen minutes. Please allow enough time to clean up after yourselves and use the facilities."

I reached into my crumpled lunch bag and pulled things out one at a time. One slightly smooshed egg salad sandwich, a bag of Fritos, and a Capri Sun.

No special treat from Mom after all.

I pulled off the top piece of bread, confirming my earlier suspicion. Mom was an ace with peanut butter and jelly (heavy on the PB) and basically everything else. She never seemed to get egg salad the way I liked it.

"What's the matter?" Other John asked.

"Too much mustard and not enough mayo." I shrugged. "Oh well."

I stabbed the straw into the silver juice pouch.

"I've got you," John said.

He dug through the pockets on his vest and started pulling out all kinds of stuff. Some were cool: a glittery, ten-sided die from the right chest pocket and a tiny Rubik's cube. Others seemed like useless junk: a handful of paper clips, various buttons, and a handful of crayon tips.

I'd sucked down half my drink and finished my corn chips by the time he found what he was looking for. A silver packet of mayo.

"Here you go."

As I reached for it, he pulled it back slightly.

"The first one's free."

"Uhh... Thanks?"

I spread out a thin layer of mayo and was about to dig in when I noticed the misshapen white lump in the box before Akira.

"What's that?"

Her eyes narrowed and locked on to Other John's. Nobody answered my question.

I looked between the two of them.

"Onigiri," Akira said, watching Other John like a hawk.

"What's onigiri?"

"Rice balls with salmon." She pointed her finger at Other John. "Don't say it!"

His cheeks puffed out, and for a moment, I thought he'd burst.

"I never knew rice had balls," Other John blurted out. He exploded into a fit of laughter, nearly hitting his head on the table.

I giggled. Akira didn't seem amused, so I let it taper off quickly.

Other John nudged me with his elbow. "Come on… that was hilarious."

Park shook his head. "Not when you've heard it almost every week for three years."

John finally controlled his laughter in time for the final announcement.

"This is your last chance to use the restrooms," the guide's voice said from somewhere behind me. "Then we'll head upstairs for everyone's favorite exhibit. The dinosaurs."

"Can I tag along with you guys?"

"Of course," Other John said.

I loaded trash into my empty lunch bag with a smile. Things were finally looking up. As I stood up to find the trash can, I realized the bag still had some weight to it. Maybe Mom didn't let me down.

My fingers immediately recognized the shape of my favorite cheese snack. She found another Babybel after all.

I turned the bag upside down. The wheel of cheese thunked onto the pile of corn chip dust. Yes, I know. Red flag four hundred. Cheese shouldn't thunk.

Nor was that the only odd thing.

There was no cellophane, and the color of the wax was all wrong. Instead of fire-engine red, it was more orange with a rough feel to it. All-in-all, it seemed more like the homemade beeswax candles Mom whipped up for craft shows than anything edible.

"Uhh... John," said Park. "Your cheese looks sick."

"My sister Leyla threw away the last Babybel. This must be something fancier."

I turned the cheese over in my hands. Problem one: it didn't have one of those little paper strips. That led to the second problem. My fingernails couldn't even dent the surface.

People stood up all around us, packing up their lunch boxes, throwing out garbage, and running off to the bathroom.

The twins got to their feet, too.

"Just throw it out," Park said.

Akira stared at her brother. "I've seen you eat a piece of pizza out of the garbage before."

"That was one time. And it was just the crust."

I kept fiddling with the wax. "It's been one of those days that only cheese can fix."

Other John fished an eyeglass repair kit from one of his many pockets.

"Here."

I drew the tiny screwdriver across the surface. The thin piece of metal made no more progress than my nail.

"Let it go, dude..." Akira said.

But there was no way I'd let this weird wheel of cheese defeat me. I readjusted, grabbing the screwdriver like a dagger.

Stinging pain shot up my arm as my hand slammed against the table.

The disembodied wails of the damned wafted out of the hole as a chunk of wax flew across the room.

CHAPTER 6
CURSE: IT'S WHAT'S FOR DINNER

Sure, someone else will tell you the screaming came from my new friends. It wasn't that. Those screams were definitely from something otherworldly. And they were just another in an extensive list of warnings I somehow missed.

Other John's and Park's faces scrunched up as they held their breath. Akira gagged and pinched her nose.

"That is rancid," she said. "Throw it out."

"Blue cheese has a strong odor and people love it," I said staring at the shattered bits of cheese strewn across the table. They were more like bits of crystal from those break-your-own-geode kits than anything edible. But Mom promised a treat.

"Do *you* love blue cheese?"

Hmm... I couldn't ever remember trying blue cheese.

"That doesn't matter," Park said, finally taking a breath. "That's not blue cheese. It smells worse than our dog's butt."

He coughed. "Oh God, it's in my nostrils."

Akira stood and backed away from the table. "Throw it out."

"Eat it," Other John said. "I dare you."

"Eww..." the twins said together. I pinched a pea-sized chunk between my fingers. The smell wafted closer. Akira and her brother retreated to the garbage cans.

Other John stood his ground, waiting for me to complete the dare.

How bad could it be?

I closed my eyes, dropped the cheese on my tongue, and instantly gagged.

It had both the consistency *and* flavor of playground sand that a neighborhood of feral cats had used as a litter box for months. (At least I assumed. I've never tasted cat turds before.)

I coughed and tried to spit the piece out. Defying gravity and logic, the chunk of cheese went to the worst place possible.

Down my throat.

I grabbed the silver juice pouch and squeezed. There wasn't even a drop inside. I looked around for something else. Anything else.

My eyes locked on the mayo packet. It beat cat poo. The tiny glob of remaining mayo wasn't enough. The aftertaste was still strong in my mouth.

"Gross," Other John said, heading to the garbage.

I swept all the crumbs off the table into my bag and tossed it in the nearby can.

"I'm not sure that was cheese."

Akira handed me a plastic bottle of water. "I told you."

I took the remaining swig and tossed it.

"Thanks."

Mrs. Barwick clapped. "Everybody ready?"

She ushered us away from the lunchroom and into the stairwell.

Every step up the stairs grew increasingly difficult. Halfway, it turned to agony. My muscles ached. Saliva filled my mouth like right before you vomited.

The room spun, and I teetered on the step. My legs gave out, and I started headfirst down the stairs.

Luckily, that terrible falling sensation didn't last long. Stephen finally proved his worth and shoved me back upright.

"Thanks..." As the word escaped my lips, something sharp stabbed me in the gut.

I grabbed my belly and froze. This wasn't a normal pain.

"We're even now."

"What do you mean?" I mumbled, holding my stomach as a second wave of cramps gripped me.

"Your Oreos fell out of your bag on the bus. They were delicious," he added with a laugh before walking away.

The gears in my head whirred so quickly I could hear them. Have you ever seen a movie with a flashback sequence? One revealing something super important that the main character either missed or couldn't possibly know? I swear that happened.

One minute, I stood in the stairwell, and the next I was looking down on myself in the ancient Egypt exhibit. Stephen stood there with that evil look in his eye. I wanted to stop him, but without a body, it was impossible.

Instead, I watched as Stephen knocked me into the display case.

I won't bore you with the recap. The important part was what happened after. Specifically, the tan, wax-covered wheel of cheese that fell from the vase and accidentally wound up in my lunch bag.

The Egyptian wing of the museum disappeared, and the stairwell materialized around me again.

Other John was behind me with his hands up, making sure I didn't collapse again. Park stood in front of me, waving his hand over my eyes.

"Are you okay?" asked Akira.

"No," I said. "I just ate three-thousand-year-old cheese."

Park looked at his sister. "What?"

"The cheese..." I blinked and saw the little tan puck burned inside my eyelids. Along with the faintest outline of the eye of Horus (I put one in the chapter heading if you want to see what it looks like).

"It came out of the vase." I pointed at Park. "And then you put it in my lunch bag."

"What? No. I." His face grew red. "Uh oh."

Lightning sharp pain pierced my stomach, sending me to my knees.

Park grabbed my arm, stabilizing me. "This is all my fault."

"Yeah, but I dared him to eat it," Other John added. "Now he's totally cursed."

"No," Akira said. "He's totally food poisoned."

She turned to me. "You should go to the bathroom and puke that out."

The idea of shoving a finger down my throat made my stomach churn further. But Akira was right. Following Dad's bad fish experiment last year, the whole family got sick. But it didn't set in for an hour. If I threw up, I could still get ahead of this.

Sweat beaded on my forehead as I scanned the crowd for a teacher. Only there wasn't time.

A different sensation brewed in my tummy. Something the *opposite* of vomit.

I tore off down the hall. And by that, I mean I galloped while crouched, over trying desperately not to poop myself. Only, I didn't know where the bathroom was.

Half a dozen wobbly steps later, the sign came into view. I never thought I'd be so happy to see those little white stick figures.

I stumbled inside the large restroom. Other than the pounding of my heartbeat and the gurgling in my stomach, the room was quiet. The lights were on this time, but the place seemed vacant.

Thank God. What followed would be unholy.

My backpack slipped to the floor as I pulled my pants down and hopped onto the first toilet.

Another wave of pain flooded my stomach. I clenched my eyes shut to keep away the tears.

Akira was wrong. This wasn't food poisoning. Something in my body needed to come out.

My gallbladder? (Not that I knew what a gallbladder was. Or where to find it.)

Appendix? My older cousin had his removed a few months ago. Was that genetic?

Then it happened. I farted. My stomach instantly felt a million times better.

I peeked out of one eye.

Gas? All that pain because of a little gas? But that terrible pain returned just as quickly as it left.

I grunted and released more gas.

It worked. Pressure built up, and I relieved it. No big deal.

But after five minutes of this, it was clear it wasn't stopping anytime soon.

I clamped my eyes shut and pushed as hard as possible.

A deafening blast surely heard all the way in the Egyptian exhibit reverberated throughout the bathroom. My ears rang.

I took a deep breath and instantly regretted it. The stench brought more tears than the pain. Rotten eggs, skunk spray, and a hint of hot garbage.

When I glanced between my legs, there was nothing solid in the bowl. Good, because I needed fresh air.

That's when I saw it.

Him...

King Tut, easily recognizable by his golden headdress and that pointy, black beard thingy. His translucent form rose from the toilet bowl and floated before me in the stall.

I froze, not believing my eyes. That's when the pharaoh grinned and reached out a ghostly hand.

CHAPTER 7
KING OF THE TOOTS

I'm not too proud to say I screamed. No, wait. "Screamed" wasn't a fair enough description of the sound that left my lips. We're talking record-breaking. A scream to end all screams. Something that rivaled a jet engine.

If somehow my colossal fart hadn't reached the ears of everyone in the museum, my banshee's wail certainly did.

My mouth hung open, but the scream trailed off. The ghost had me paralyzed, and unable to produce any further sound. In addition, it left me oblivious to the footsteps entering the restroom.

"Are you okay?" the male teacher I'd never put a name to asked. "Oh. Oh, God," he added before choking on my farts.

I wanted to scream, to say anything, but I still couldn't find my voice. The ghost possessed some power that rooted me in place.

A singular thought ran through my mind.

The curse was real. And I'm going to die on the toilet in a public restroom.

My eyes fixated on a golden piece of armor on Tut's pointer finger. A sharp, metal claw inching toward my eyeball.

"Do you need help?" The teacher's voice faltered as he fought not to breathe in the foul gas heavy in the room.

Tutankhamun didn't care a teacher was outside the stall. He was going to kill me regardless.

Tears streamed down my face.

My teacher's fist pounded on the stall door, freeing me from my paralysis. I threw my hand in front of my face and jerked away. Of course, I lost my balance and fell onto the cold floor. (I know... Eww. But it kept me from King Tut's grasp, so I didn't complain.)

However, the sound of my scrawny, bare butt hitting the floor only caused further alarm.

The entire stall rattled under his fist, and the lock dislodged. The door swung open and slammed against the adjacent wall.

Mr. Whatshisname stared in equal parts concern and disgust. His face flushed red as he spotted my shorts around my ankles. He gasped, choking on the lingering stink, and covered his eyes.

It took me a few seconds to realize King Tut's ghost was gone. It had dissipated as the door passed *through* him. I was safe. Well, as safe as I could be at that moment.

"What happened?" The teacher coughed and gagged again.

"I'm fine. Get out!"

I kicked the door shut (which naturally bounced right back open).

"Okay," he said before leaving fast enough to leave a dust cloud behind. Though, maybe it was just the gas hanging in the air.

I pulled up my shorts as another bout of nausea gripped my stomach. Luckily, I hadn't left the toilet yet.

Vomit spewed from my mouth like an angry fire hose. Honestly, I was at ease with this. It was the reason I'd come here anyway. Bits of egg salad sandwich and chewed chips coated the wall and the toilet until my lunch, and quite likely my soul, left my body.

For the record, that tiny speck of cheese tasted no better coming up.

"Still okay in there?" the teacher yelled from outside the restroom.

"Yeah," I lied.

I stumbled to the sink and rinsed my mouth. The mirror showed how pale my face had gone. It was understandable after everything that had exited my body.

The hallucination of King Tut suddenly made sense. It had to be from toxic cheese mold. But it was definitely out of my system now.

Hopefully.

I ran water over my face again, toweled it off, and stepped out of the restroom.

My face went from flush to red in about a second. Not only was the teacher standing there, but also my new friends. All looked equally horrified at what they'd heard (and/or smelled).

"I uhh..." Mr. Whatshisname's eyes focused on the wall behind me. "Think we should go to the nurse." He looked down at the clipboard in his hand. "John Pahrsink, right?"

"More like Fartstink." Butt-crack Steve stepped out from behind the teacher and raised his arm for a high-five. He snorted when nobody slapped his hand and let it fall to his side. "You *all* stink."

"That's enough, Stephen," the man said in a voice that more resembled an angry father than a teacher. "Return to the group."

He pointed down the hall.

"That goes for all of you."

Other John's hands bridged over his vest, searching for the appropriate pockets. "There's some vomit on your shirt," he said, passing me a napkin and a mostly crushed packet of Saltines.

With manly nods, he and Park turned around and headed back.

I doubled over as another wave of pain hit. The good news? It didn't last nearly as long as any of the other cramps.

The bad news? I farted right in front of Akira without thinking.

"Feel better," she said, already hurrying away.

"Feel better," mocked Butt-crack Steve.

"Now, Stephen," the teacher said.

My bully finally turned around and walked off.

I'm not sure if it was the noxious fumes, but the trip to the first aid station was a blur. All I remember is sounding like a duck the entire trip and the teacher's knuckles rapped against the door.

A larger bubble rose in my stomach. And of course, another bout of gas escaped. Louder than the others and stinking to high heaven.

I glanced behind me, hoping nobody was in the back blast. Luckily, the corridor was mostly clear.

When I turned around, I saw it again.

That menacing translucent face of King Tut. His golden headdress glowed beneath the fluorescent lights. My voice caught in my throat again as he opened a cavernous mouth.

It was definitely the curse.

King Tut had come to swallow my soul for eating his cheese.

CHAPTER 8
A DEADLY DIAGNOSIS

[Insert terrifying mummy speech here]

You're probably thinking right about now that the brackets above are some kind of placeholder from the first draft of this book. That I'm a lousy author and forgot to replace it. It's not, I'm not, and I didn't.

King Tut was a ruler from ancient **Egypt**. Nobody spoke English back then. I couldn't translate whatever syllables came out of that thing's ghastly lips, much less know what hieroglyphs to use for them.

I screamed and dove backward, slamming my shoulder into the floor in the same spot where Stephen had walloped me earlier. But that pain was nothing compared to the lifelong knowledge that I'd just sacrificed my teacher to one of the undead.

I wish I could tell you the sound of King Tut siphoning a man's soul straight from his lips wouldn't haunt me forever. Actually, I guess I *can* tell you that because it didn't happen.

The door to the medical room flung open and a nurse who looked suspiciously like another old, white-haired museum volunteer, stepped into the hall.

He looked at my teacher, then they both stared down at me, waiting for an explanation I couldn't provide.

King Tut might not have swallowed anyone's soul, but he sure made me look like a fool.

Neither of them saw the ghost, even though it was practically on top of them. I *was* cursed. But of course, I couldn't explain without any of that admitting to vandalizing museum property.

"Ow. I, uh..." I said, stalling for time. "There was a mouse." I pointed past their legs and got to my feet.

"Every building in the city has mice," said the 'medical professional.' "But they don't eat much. Come inside and tell me what's ailing you, besides your musophobia?"

"Huh?" I said, following my teacher inside.

I took some baby steps and braced myself for the ghost nobody else could see to burst out to scare the bajesus out of me again.

There was no sign of my stinky specter.

"Musophobia," the volunteer repeated, slapping the top of a padded wooden bench. "The fear of mice. Take a seat. Do you need some ice?"

I checked behind the door. Nothing.

I was too busy peering under the bench to hear what the old man said, but there was nothing there either.

Of course not, dummy. King Tut's a ghost, and ghosts can pass through walls.

"John," my teacher said.

I stood back up. "Huh?"

"He asked if you wanted some ice for your shoulder?"

I moved my arm in a circle. There'd probably be a bruise tomorrow, but it didn't hurt. "No. I'm fine." I rechecked the four corners of the room. Still no sign of the ghost.

The volunteer patted the bench again. "Come on, son. The mice won't bite, and neither do I."

My hesitation prompted Mr. Whatshisface to take the lead.

"I'm Mr... Sorry." He shook his head. "Force of habit with the kids. Just Walter. And this is John."

"Howie," the white-haired man said with a smile.

"John's been having some. Well..." He coughed. "Gastrointestinal distress."

"Something you ate, maybe?"

I groaned. "You could say that."

"Hydration is the best thing for food poisoning. Maybe some Pepto." He tilted his head toward the bench beside him.

I peered around for King Tut one last time, then jumped onto the bench. Naturally, farting when I landed.

Howie took half a step back, faced my teacher, and wrinkled his nose. "I see what you mean. That is potent." He turned back toward me. "Do you know what you ate?"

I shook my head but couldn't help whispering under my breath. "Only three-thousand-year-old cheese belonging to King Tut."

"That would certainly do it," Howie said with a chuckle (he apparently had his hearing aid set to eleven).

I froze. "This has happened before?"

"Oh yeah. It happens in the museum all the time."

I scooted forward on the bench and gave him my full attention. "How do I break the curse?"

"Watch what you eat. At my age, I can't even look at beans. Metabolism is wasted on the youth."

My shoulders sank, taking any traces of hope along with them.

My stomach churned. I clenched my teeth and held my breath.

"Cramping?" he asked, watching my cheeks turn red.

I nodded and did my best to contain it. The ghost seemed to appear every time I farted loudly.

"Well, don't hold it in, son," Howie said, retreating to the other side of the room.

Mr. Just-Walter quickly backed up as well.

The old man smiled and tapped his temple. "Better to be a smart feller than a fart smeller."

I burst out laughing. And something else burst out too, if you catch my drift.

The pain in my stomach abated. I checked my surroundings. No pain and no ghost.

Howie cocked his head. "Better?"

I nodded, now holding my breath for a different reason.

"I'll, uh, just give you a moment to air out and then I'll come take your temperature."

He smiled and drummed his fingers against his leg. "Do you have a favorite part of the museum so far?"

I shrugged. *Definitely NOT ancient Egypt.*

"Not much for small talk. That's okay."

I smiled. It didn't last long as an ache settled into my lungs. I shut my eyes and braced for the stench.

My nose picked up nothing. At that moment, I realized something. The ghost had nothing to do with "regular" farts. It showed up with the stinky ones.

Gears turned in my head. Howie and Mr. Just-Walter didn't share my curse. They couldn't see the ghost because they hadn't eaten Tut's nasty old cheese.

My brain was on a roll. But it didn't stop there.

King Tut wasn't just any old ghost. He was a ghost made of farts. King Toot! When you fart, your natural reaction is to wave it away. It was the air movement from the door that dispersed him. The same thing had happened in the bathroom stall.

There were still some logistical issues. Mainly, I couldn't tell the ghost-summoning farts from the regular while they were in my belly. But knowing I could smell them was at least a start.

I sat a little taller, confident this newfound knowledge would keep me safe until I broke the curse.

"I see you're feeling better already," said Howie. "As long as your temperature checks out, I think you can rejoin your classmates."

He took a tentative step toward me, verified the air as clear, and stuck a digital thermometer in my ear.

"Ninety-nine." He stepped away and set it down on the countertop. "Keep hydrated and you'll be right as rain in no time."

"That's it?" I asked. "You can't give me any medicine? Beano? Pepto?"

"Food poisoning needs to run its course. Besides, you want to push the poison out, not keep it in."

Easy for you to say. You're not farting out ancient Egyptian rulers.

Mr. Just-Walter checked the digital clock on the wall. "We're scheduled to leave in about an hour. I'm happy to call your parents and let them know you're ill, but it might take them that long to get here."

I lowered my head. Dad's allergic to big cities and driving on the highway gives mom anxiety. Besides, I was sure the solution to breaking the curse lived within the museum. Which meant I had an hour to find it.

"I'd like to continue the tour," I said.

My teacher smiled. "Good. Nobody ever got hurt over a little fart."

"Well..." Howie said. "If you're a history buff, that's not entirely true."

My breath caught in my throat. "What?"

He laughed. "A fart caused a rather bloody rebellion in ancient Egypt. But those times are long gone. You have nothing to worry about."

I gulped. "What exactly happened?"

"It's a rather long story, but here's the gist of it. People grew tired of their king and appointed one of his trusted allies to take over. When the king sent another of his generals to deal with him, the would-be usurper farted in his direction and told him to bring it back to the king." Howie laughed again. "As you can imagine, it didn't go over well."

I faked a laugh, which, in hindsight, was a terrible idea. Even that slight chuckle proved too much for my delicate digestive tract. An old trombone sound reverberated throughout the small, windowless room. The stench of rotten eggs hit my nostrils.

I gagged for a moment before holding my breath. That stench meant one thing.... My head whipped back and forth. King Toot wouldn't be far behind.

Howie coughed and shuffled back, waving his hand in a feeble attempt to clear the air.

Mr. Just-Walter stayed on the opposite side of the room. Though the wrinkles of his face said he wasn't far enough downwind for his liking.

I glanced left and right. We were the only people in the room. So much for my earlier theory of 'The stink following ghost.'

My lungs ached, forcing me to suck in a breath, smell or not. That was my second mistake. The first being when I only checked the *corners* of the room. Farts don't travel diagonally.

King Toot's face bent down from above me, twisting at an

angle only possible for a ghost. His empty, hollow eyes stared into my very soul. At least right up to the point where I inhaled him.

Everything went black. I had the distinct feeling of falling. I threw my hands out to the side, bracing for an impact that never came.

The whooshing of air around me died down. Darkness gave way to a blinding light that burned my eyes and face alike. The air was clean and fresh. Not a single trace of methane.

I squinted into a deep blue sky where the sun blazed. My hand passed through something soft and flowing as I sat up.

"What the..."

Pyramids dotted the sandy horizon. Farting out ghosts wasn't the worst thing the curse had to offer.

CHAPTER 9
A BLAST FROM THE PAST

My breath came out in ragged fits. I'd been here for only a few seconds and sweat already poured from my forehead. I was too pale for this. There was no way I'd survive in ancient Egypt without sunscreen. Not to mention food, water, or television.

There had to be a way back to the museum.

I jumped to my feet and turned in a slow circle. An endless sea of sand and stone stretched as far as the eye could see.

A shadow blocked out the sun. I spun around and found myself face to face with King Tut. This one wasn't translucent or floating. It was the actual King Tutankhamun.

This was the honest to God Egyptian ruler of old: tan skin, golden headdress reflecting the sun like a disco ball, expensive bejeweled scepter.

I looked around again. *This is ancient Egypt.*

It didn't seem like King Tut wanted my soul. I was helpless here. He could have just taken it.

Or maybe Toot did, but Tut didn't. They felt like two completely different people.

"What do you want with me?" I asked.

"ركع, لص," his voice boomed.

More stuff you can't understand. I know, it's probably frustrating. But I felt that if I pulled the bracket thing a second time, you really WOULD think I'm a lousy author.

Just bear with me, okay? Everything eventually becomes clear.

"What?"

He pointed his scepter at me.

"سوف تخدمني يا أوشابتي."

I threw my arms in the air. "I don't understand what you're saying."

King Tutankhamun growled something else unintelligible and raised his scepter to the heavens. The wind picked up. Sand whipped around me, stinging my eyes and blotting out the sun.

At the center of it, Egypt's teenage ruler pulled his arms down. The wind changed direction and dragged me backwards through the desert. I looked over my shoulder. A sarcophagus raced toward me from the opposite direction, ready to swallow me up.

I fell backward, and my bottom hit the bench with a faint thump.

"John?" Howie said, holding out a bottle of water in his hand. "Where'd you go?"

I blinked and shook the cobwebs from my head. The hot sun, pyramids, sand—all of it was gone. In their place were more unanswerable questions.

What was that?

Did King Toot possess me? Did he take my soul?

Was that one of his memories?

Finally, and most importantly, would this happen every time the ghost touched me?

"Ushabti." The word snuck from my lips without conscious thought.

"What's that?"

"What?" I said, taking the water from Howie. It was ice cold and wonderful. I pulled the top off and greedily downed the entire bottle.

"You just said 'Ushabti'."

Hearing the word aloud a second time triggered my memory. It was the one thing King Tut had said that I could understand. Well, not understand exactly, more like could pronounce.

"Ushabti," I said again. "It was on a sign in the Egyptian exhibit. Do you know what it means?"

"Not my area of expertise, I'm afraid. But the museum is open seven days a week except Thanksgiving and Christmas.

"You're welcome back. But maybe leave the digestive problems at home next time."

He gave a polite smile before walking over to my teacher.

I glanced up at the clock. Barely any time had passed since my impromptu Egypt trip. However, there wasn't much time before the bus left. ↳ Unplanned

Ushabti, I thought. *Ushabti means something important, if only I could figure out what.*

My eyes lit up. I already had the tool to figure it out. I reached into my backpack and found the pocket translator.

But it wouldn't power on.

That's right... Butt-crack Steve had knocked one of the batteries out on the bus.

My eyes settled on the digital thermometer sitting on the counter a few feet away. Bingo.

I hopped off the bench and slipped across the room while the adults whispered to one another. Making sure my back was to them, I pretended to drink from the empty bottle. My other hand slid open the battery compartment and pried the battery free.

The plastic bottle went into the trash can beside the counter, the cover went back on the thermometer, and nobody was wiser. It was the perfect crime. And just in time.

Mr. Just-Walter faced me. "Let's get you back to the rest of the group before we miss our ride home."

I slipped the battery into my pocket and joined his side.

"Thank you for your help," Mr. Just-Walter said.

"Yeah, thanks," I echoed.

Howie shrugged. "Can't say I did much, but I hope you feel better."

"Me too."

As I stepped past him, he leaned close and winked. "Blame your horrendous farts on your teacher. It's what I'd do if I were your age."

I smiled even though I knew it wouldn't work. Stephen had been present for the 'bathroom incident' and I'm sure he'd blabbed to everyone already.

We trudged through the museum's halls and into the Evolving Planet exhibit. Displays held colorful stones. The stones gave way to fossils of small sea creatures. And those to larger animals.

The larger animals got larger and larger until we found the museum's most famous piece. Sue, the tyrannosaurus rex. But not just any T-Rex—the largest, most complete one in existence.

Or at least, her skull, safely encased in glass and surrounded by a crowd of museumgoers.

For a moment, I completely forgot about my curse and the fact that I was supposed to be following Mr. Just-Walter back to my classmates. It was just me and a fossilized skull as large as me.

I pushed through the crowd and leaned over the display. Dozens of sharp teeth as long as my fingers lined Sue's jaw.

"Wow." My breath fogged up the glass.

I glanced over at a nearby mural of the creature, its ferocious mouth opened wide, showing all the other dinosaurs it was the boss.

But there was more (a lot more).

My feet carried me to the next room where the rest of Sue's body towered over me.

According to the nearby signage, this skull was a fake. The authentic noggin was too heavy, so they kept it in the case where it was easier studied. But even the fake one was cool.

Staring up at the dozens of giant rib bones, my mind went somewhere morbid. I wondered how many children would fit in the beast's belly. Somewhere between two and four. At least, if she didn't chew.

It was a shame Sue wasn't alive. And an even bigger shame she didn't eat Butt-crack Steve before he knocked over that jar and set the curse in motion.

The thought of Butt-crack Steve ended my childish daydream. Sue was cool, and I mean, *really* cool, but I was wasting time. I had a curse to break.

Crap. Now I had to find the chaperone I'd wandered away from, too.

I spun around in a panic and that problem solved itself. Mr. Just-Walter was only a few feet away, watching me admire the T-Rex.

"Sorry," I said with a gasp.

"I used to love dinosaurs, too," he said, nodding toward Sue. "Do you want to look around some more? I can give you another five minutes."

I shook my head. Howie didn't know that Egyptian word, but I bet our proper tour guide might. "No. I'd like to get back to my friends."

We found our group through a corridor of dinosaur skeletons. I caught Other John's fisherman vest through the sail of a Dimetrodon on the other side of the room.

Akira turned at that moment and waved.

Walking toward the group, I realized I never considered how (or what) to tell my new friends. They deserved the truth. Plus, I couldn't do this alone.

"Welcome back, Fartstink."

Of course, Butt-crack Steve had followed my friends.

"Ignore him," Akira said, shuffling forward with the group. "Are you feeling any better?"

"No. Not really."

My ears perked up as our tour guide offered to field questions. I shot my hand up but didn't wait for him to call on me.

"Can we go back to the Egyptian section after this?"

Mrs. Barwick appeared from behind some other students. "We only have time to pop into the gift shop and use the restrooms before we return to the bus."

The volunteer smiled. "Any other questions?"

"Yeah," I called out again. "Can you tell us more about King Tut? And his curses?"

"Umm... Any questions about the Evolving Planet Exhibit?"

A boy in front raised his hand. "How much—"

"What does 'Ushabti' mean?" I shouted over the other kid.

"Uhh... John," Akira said.

I ignored her, and the fact that Mrs. Barwick was heading in our direction.

"Has anyone in the museum been cursed by any of the artifacts here?"

"That's enough," said our teacher. "If you're that obsessed with the Egypt exhibit, you can prepare a report for the class tomorrow."

"Ooh. Busted," Stephen whispered from somewhere behind me.

The teacher eyed him, too, and he quickly shut his mouth.

Meanwhile, my stomach bottomed out. Just anxiety, though. I couldn't remember a single thing from the tour (aside from King Tut's penchant for cursing people with horrendous farts).

My new friends circled around me as other kids rattled off actual questions about dinosaurs.

"What's going on, John?" Akira said.

Other John raised a finger. "Other John. He's Other John, remember?"

Akira and Park shook their heads and said "nope" in unison.

He whined, but Akira ignored him and went on.

"Why are you asking about curses?"

"Because I'm cursed." The words spilled from my mouth, but my hands did their fair share of the talking. "That cheese wasn't from my mom. It was inside the urn. King Tut's urn. Now my farts summon his ghost."

The three of them stared at me for a moment and then looked at each other.

"We told you that cheese smelled funky, but you're not cursed. You'll be fine in a few days."

"It's not food poisoning." I tried stomping my foot dramatically, but it only triggered another bout of gas. I clutched my belly. Something told me this one wouldn't be pretty.

I'll just say it burned coming out and leave it at that.

Dinosaur bones rattled and a nearby seismic sensor chirped an alarm.

My classmates laughed.

And then the smell hit.

Someone started sobbing, several others screamed, at least one person vomited, and a few kids received scrapes and bruises as their peers trampled them.

My poor friends remained by my side at the epicenter of the blast. I focused on the floor and held my breath.

None of them said a word, and I couldn't hold my breath any longer.

"I am so sorry..."

I glanced up. My friends stared past me, motionless. They wouldn't so much as look me in the eye.

"Guys?"

Nobody blinked. Great. My fart had paralyzed them.

Other John's arm crept upwards, shaking the entire time. "What in the ever-living heck is that?"

CHAPTER 10

MINOR SEWAGE LEAKS

Park shook free of his stupor first and jumped into action. He slipped his backpack off one shoulder and swung it in a wide arc.

"Don't let it touch you!" I shouted, backing away.

It was too late. The bag passed right through the ghost. Park lost his footing and went along with it. He fell through the translucent Egyptian ruler and hit the marble floor.

Perfect.

I backpedaled further and knocked over one of those gold stands that keep you away from the artifacts.

King Toot wafted closer.

Akira rushed to the aid of her twin. She looked back at me. "What happens if he touches you?"

"You get stuck in ancient Egypt."

I scurried to the other side of the Dimetrodon.

It did no good.

"Ushabti," the ghost said as he flowed between the dinosaur's bones.

What happened if he touched me again? Would I get stuck longer? Is this a 'three strikes and you're out' thing? Would two more touches trap me there forever?

Other John ran toward me.

I waved my hands. "Stay back."

"I've got this," he said, digging in his pockets as he ran.

He didn't have this.

Other John's foot caught the velvet rope, and he tripped.

He fell in slow motion, but it was a thing of beauty. He managed to twist his body midair and land on his back. That flimsy fabric vest of his slid across the polished floor like an air hockey puck. Right toward King Toot...

I closed my eyes. I couldn't watch the ghost take another one of my friends.

"Eat this, fart face!" my friend screamed.

I peeked in time to see Other John hold out a tiny spray bottle and hammer down the nozzle.

Vague floral notes filled the air.

King Toot kept coming. "Ushab—" and then he just sort of... dissolved.

Other John pumped his fist. "Hah!"

I squinted, looking for any sign of my ghost, but came up empty. He took King Toot down with... an air freshener?

Other John lay there on his back below me. "Well, aren't you going to help me up?"

I blinked and helped my friend to his feet.

"How... How'd you know to do that?"

Other John shrugged. "How'd you *not*? He's a fart."

I opened my mouth to explain how normal kids don't carry perfume around but decided against it. After all, he sorta saved my life.

My head snapped toward ground zero. "Park!"

We both ran over to him, Other John spritzing the air along the way.

"Are you okay?"

"No." He spat onto the floor. "Your stupid fart ghost got in my mouth."

"But... You didn't go anywhere?"

Park shook his head.

We all turned toward a loud whistle, where a man in a museum security uniform waved his arms.

"Attention. There's been a break in the main sewer line. Please make your way out through the lobby."

Butt-crack Steve yelled from somewhere among the chaos. "Nuh uh. The sewer is the new kid's butt."

"There's no way that smell could have come from a person," Akira said.

The other students seemed to accept that. Or at least they didn't stare at me.

Mrs. Barwick's voice was all nasally from her holding her nose with one hand. "If there's no objection, we'll skip the visit to the gift shop and head outside."

Everyone nodded and hurried along. Breathable air trumped cheap plastic trinkets anytime.

Our teachers and museum tour guides herded us back down the stairwell. The smell trailed alongside us, though somewhat muted compared to before. By the time we hit the great outdoors, it was gone, and I breathed easily.

Well, we all breathed more easily.

Mrs. Barwick ushered us away from the closed doors of the empty bus.

"We still have some time before our departure. Please stick together."

I sat down on the steps. My friends followed suit.

"You really are cursed," Akira said.

"That's what I was trying to tell you. And I'm sure my best bet for breaking the curse lies back there."

"Air freshener took care of him," said Other John.

"Temporarily. A sudden burst of wind does the same. But next time I fart, he'll be back." I took a deep breath. "Thanks."

Akira looked around. "For what?"

"Oh, you didn't hear?" Other John beamed and pointed his thumbs at his chest. "I saved his life."

"Not just that. Thanks for being able to see him. It's nice knowing I'm not crazy." I scratched an itch on my nose. "Wait. How come you guys can see him? None of the teachers or other kids could."

"Maybe it's because we all smelled that stinky cheese."

Everyone but Akira bobbed their heads.

"I don't think that's it." She turned to her brother. "What happened when you touched him, Park?"

He shook his head. "Nothing."

"John said his touch would send you to Egypt. It didn't work on you because he's the only one cursed."

"*Other* John," Other John muttered.

"Seriously, let it go." Akira slapped his arm. "What was I saying?"

"That only John is cursed," Park said. He frowned and looked at me. "Sorry, John."

"We're the ones who accidentally put the cheese in your lunch. Though none of this was our fault. If there were any fairness in the world, it'd be Stephen with the curse."

The four of us sat on the steps in silence for a few minutes.

"Look at the bright side," Other John said. "At least you're not peeing ghosts."

"Stop!" the rest of us cried in unison.

It took another few minutes for me to rid myself of *that* mental image.

"So... Do any of you have experience breaking curses?" Unsurprisingly, nobody spoke up. "What about the word 'Ushabti'?"

More noes and head shakes.

I sighed. At least I had a way to fight back against King Toot thanks to Other John.

"Wait!" I dug the battery from my pocket. My heart sank. "Ugh. It's a triple-A. My translator takes doubles."

Other John reached into his left breast pocket. "How many do you need?"

"Just one."

He held it just out of reach. "Batteries are a dollar apiece."

I blinked. Was he serious?

"Just give it to him," Akira said.

"These supplies come from my own allowance. I'm a business, not a charity."

"What if he traded you for it? His triple for your double?"

Other John sighed. "Fine."

"It better have juice," I said after making the swap.

"All sales are final."

I plugged it into the device, leaving it inside my backpack to shield it from the teachers (and Butt-crack Steve).

Bingo. The screen came to life, ready to satisfy all my translating needs. I took my best guess at spelling 'Ushabti,' but it made no difference.

There was no option to translate from Egyptian.

"So," Akira said. "What does it mean?"

"Nothing. Egyptian is a dead language."

"Try Arabic."

A few button presses later and we had our answer.

Or not. *Ushabti.*

I sighed. "Ushabti means Ushabti. Of course it does." I wouldn't find out more until I got home and onto the family computer.

Just then, the driver walked past us and opened the door to the bus.

As I gathered my things and jumped up, something cold and wet hit the back of my arm. I spun around and found Other John with the air freshener canister.

"What? We're stuck on this bus for the next hour. I'm not taking any chances."

"Okay." I gave a reluctant nod. "That's fair."

I wiped my hand on my pants and followed my friends onboard. Stephen was far behind us. At least I didn't have to deal with him on the ride back.

"You can sit with me," Other John said.

Whether he really wanted to sit with me or continue to coat me with air freshener was anyone's guess.

Honestly, I didn't care (as long as I wasn't paying per spray).

The bus started up, and the students filed in. Whatever relief was short-lived as Stephen took the empty seat across from Other John and me.

He said something insulting, but my new friends ignored him and kept to themselves. Me? I watched the museum fade into the distance and daydreamed.

Howie clearly knew all along what I was really talking about. He didn't say anything in front of Mr. Just-Walter because he couldn't. He belonged to a secret society of elderly museum curators who protected the world from these kinds of problems.

King Toot couldn't follow me home because of the Coalition of Old Guys. The COG set precautions around the museum campus, making sure nothing could get out.

As we got farther from the city, my anxiety lessened. Things would be okay. Other John had doused me with perfume. That was another impenetrable barrier.

Guess what happened next?

Yup. My daydreams faded as my belly burbled with a fresh bout of gas.

I shifted in my seat, preparing to relieve the pressure and found myself staring straight into John's spray bottle.

"Do you feel lucky, punk?"

"Come on," I said, shielding my eyes. "Not in the face."

"If King Toot is coming, we must be ready."

The top of Akira and Park's heads appeared over the seat in front of us. Nosey Nellies.

Other John stared at me, waiting for an excuse to blast away.

Have you ever had someone stare at you when you had to fart? It's unnerving.

"Well, get on with it," he said.

"He doesn't show up every time," I explained. "Only with the ones that smell really bad. At least, that's my current theory."

That's when it hit me. And by 'it,' I mean Other John's palm. The force against my belly did the trick.

Pbbrt!

"Evacuate the bus!" Butt-crack Steve yelled. "Fart-Stink let another one rip."

CHAPTER 11
HE WHO SMELT IT

My friends and I were stuck with an impossible choice. Holding out breaths meant avoiding my homemade poison gas. Unfortunately, that left us prone to sneak attacks from King Toot.

Other John saw things differently. He swung his legs into the aisle and faced Stephen head on.

"Oh yeah, well, whoever smelt it, dealt it."

Butt-crack Steve narrowed his eyebrows and straightened his back.

We were in for a fight. Kids sat up in their seats like prairie dogs.

Everyone but me forgot about the danger that fart posed. But it was odorless, so we were safe. Not safe from the humiliation of ripping one on the bus, but safe in general.

"Whoever denied it, supplied it," Steve shot back.

"He who said the rhyme, did the crime."

"You just rhymed too, you idiot."

Other John wiped his hands on one another. "So, you concede?"

"What? No. He... Uh... He who thunk it, stunk it."

"He who tells of it, smells of it," Other John said without missing a beat.

Steve jutted his finger in Other John's face. "He who rapped it, crapped it."

"Whoever spoke the words, baked the turds." Other John smiled. "I can do this all day."

They went back and forth like this for a good five minutes. I honestly can't remember half the retorts, but suffice to say, most of Steve's included detention-worthy words.

I think the end of it went something like this...

"Whoever pointed the finger..." Stephen looked around, face red, forehead dotted with sweat. "Pulled their finger."

Akira raised Other John's hand in the air and the bus erupted. People chanted 'John' over and over.

Akira stared at Other John. "That was actually impressive."

"I have three older brothers and fourteen cousins—all boys. You could say I know my farts."

She stared at him for a moment. "Okay, eww... I meant the way you stood up for John."

"Oh. Well, I don't think you've ever complimented me before."

"Don't get used to it," she muttered after turning around.

Other John frowned, looked down at his lap, and seemed to only then remember the air freshener.

"Relax," I said. "It's fine."

He slipped the bottle back into one of his many pockets and pulled a book with a spy on the front out of his backpack.

I sat back against the hard, green seat and looked out the window. As the cars passed us on the highway, I tried thinking about literally anything other than my predicament. You can imagine how that went.

It was only a matter of time before King Toot returned. Lunch was two hours ago. Since then, I'd farted a couple dozen times. Three of them had summoned the ghost. If I did the math correctly (I did), that meant King Toot would show his face every forty-five minutes or so.

Dead. I was dead. I could spend all my allowance money on air freshener, and it wouldn't make a difference. I couldn't cover my butt twenty-four-seven. What if I farted in my sleep?

"Are you okay?" Other John set the book in his lap and turned toward me. "All I can hear is you chewing on your nails."

"No." I put my hand down and spit out a wad of fingernail mulch. "King Toot is gonna kill me before I can figure out how to break this curse."

Park popped up and rested his nose on the top of the seat in front of me. "Charcoal underwear."

"What?"

"My grandpa wears special underwear lined with charcoal because he has a lot of health problems. They take the smell right out of your farts."

I perked up. "Really? Are you messing with me?"

"It's true." Akira appeared beside her brother. "He used to smell almost as bad as, uhh... skunks."

Other John shook his head. "Except it doesn't stop them from smelling. It filters them. All it'll do is keep King Toot pressed right up against your—"

"Stop," the twins said together.

Other John scratched his chin. "What if you apologized?"

"Pssh," Park said. "Apologize. To a ghost."

"Wait," said Akira. "That might work."

Other John did a double take. "Really?"

"King Tut was a teenager when he died. And John's just a kid. It's not like he's a tomb raider. Sure, they speak different languages and were born three thousand years apart, but they're not that different."

She shrugged. "It couldn't hurt."

"Hey, good idea, Other John," Other John said in a high voice that sounded nothing like Akira. He touched his heart and returned to his normal pitch. "Why, thank you, Akira."

She rolled her eyes and her face disappeared behind the seat.

"Welcome to Jonathan Elementary," Park said, before we lost sight of him, too.

The upside was that my stomach held the rest of the bus ride.

We pulled up to the school, and I spotted Mom's green SUV among others of similar makes and models. I guess nobody was going home via the bus.

"We'll see you at school tomorrow, John," Akira said as we marched off the bus.

"Thanks, guys," I said with a smile. "And uh… girls."

Park and I exchanged a fist bump before he and his sister headed toward their vehicle.

Other John stared at me without a word before giving me one final spritz for the road.

"How was your—" Mom said as soon as I threw the back door open. I flung my backpack, and it hit the opposite door. Naturally, everything spilled out onto the floor.

"That good, huh?"

I slammed the door behind me and slipped on my seatbelt with a grunt.

"Do you want to talk about it?"

I stuffed my things back into my bag but couldn't find my pocket translator. Ugh. It had probably slid under the front seat.

"Well, let's see," I said as I struggled against the seatbelt to reach the device. "I got paired up with the class bully who kept getting me in trouble with the teachers and I didn't get enough time to see the dinosaur exhibit.

"Oh, and I found out the field trip was **optional**."

Plus, I fart ghosts now.

The lap belt dug into my stomach, and I abandoned the translator. I looked up and found Mom looking at me in the rearview mirror.

"You **lied**," I said.

Her mouth pulled down, and her eyes snapped back to the road.

That probably wasn't fair. Butt-crack Steve deserved my anger, not Mom.

"I wanted to give you an opportunity to learn the bus route and make some friends. Listen, I know you're upset—"

I blinked.

No. You really don't.

"But I also know how hard it is being the 'new kid.' Grandma and Grandpa moved around a lot when I was young. Five different schools in eight years. I thought the museum would offer a more relaxed setting for making friends."

We drove in silence for a few minutes.

I guessed it had worked. That had to account for something.

"I did meet some kids. Akira and her brother Park, and then another boy named John. Well, we call him Other John."

Mom's lips moved to a more neutral position, and some of the guilt I felt faded away.

"Other John?" she asked, raising an eyebrow.

"They thought it would be too confusing since we had the same name."

"If he was there first, why aren't you Other John?"

I shrugged. "He thought it was cool for about a minute. But I think the others knew it would bother him. Now they won't let him change."

"That doesn't sound nice of them, but I'm glad you made some friends."

My stomach rumbled. "What's for dinner?" I wasn't thinking about eating at this point; it was part of our usual homecoming routine.

"Enchiladas, rice, and beans."

Gulp.

Mom noticed my reaction in the mirror.

"What's with the face? I thought it was your favorite."

My stomach gurgled again. Enchiladas were my favorite. So were beans (which my family calls 'whistle-berries' on account of making your butt whistle). The problem was King Toot would love them more.

CHAPTER 12
THE FART FACT FIASCO

My family shoveled forkfuls of steaming enchiladas into their mouths. They looked amazing, all covered in delicious, creamy red sauce and dripping cheese. The food, not my family. It'd be weird if they were the ones covered in dripping cheese.

Anyway...

What awaited me following that feast wouldn't be pretty. That's why I sat there pushing a slightly burnt quesadilla triangle around my otherwise empty plate.

Dad slathered his enchilada in hot sauce. By my count, it was his third. "You're sure you just want a quesadilla?"

"I'm not hungry."

"John? Not hungry?" Leyla said. "Yeah, right. I bet he snuck a bunch of candy on his trip."

I stared at my sister. "There was a sewage leak at the museum. We ate on the bus home."

"Gross," Leyla said. "Is that why you smell?"

Mom gave her a look, then returned her attention to me. "I thought you smelled funny in the car. But more like perfume than sewage."

"Yeah. They, uh, sprayed everyone's clothes so nobody would get sick from the smell." I pushed the plate away. "May I be excused? I need to use the computer for some homework."

"Homework?" Dad said, looking back and forth between me and Mom. "On the first day of school?"

"He knows, honey."

"Oh." He stuffed another bite of food in his mouth and chewed. "Well, what kind of teacher assigns homework the day *before* the first day of school?"

I snorted. "The same kind of idiot that plans a field trip the day before the first day of school." I regretted the words the moment they left my mouth.

Mom glared at me. "Maybe they assigned the homework because you treated them like an idiot." She waved her fork in my direction. "And they'd be well within their rights."

"Sorry," I said, sinking into the chair. "I had a rough day."

Dad shook his head. "If you're skipping on enchilada night, I'd say so."

I gave my best smile complete with puppy dog eyes. "So can I be excused?"

"I suppose—" Dad started. But Mom wasn't giving in that easily.

"You can mind your manners and wait until everyone is finished," she said. "And after you've cleaned off the table and loaded the dishwasher."

I groaned but knew fighting her any further on the subject would do no good.

"But you guys said I could do a video call with my friends from Iowa," Leyla said. "They're expecting me at six."

"Oh, right." Mom turned around and checked the clock on the stove. "John gets a turn for thirty minutes, and then you can talk with your friends."

"It might take me longer than that."

Mom sighed. "Fine. Just this once you're excused. But as soon as that clock hits six, your butt's back in here doing your chores."

"Deal," I said, jumping up and rushing into the neighboring room. Honestly, I had so much to research and the presentation wasn't at the top of the list.

I fell into the creaky chair and pressed the button on top of the tower. Old fans whirred like a squadron of helicopters. A prompt on the screen blinked, awaiting a password.

"Dad! I need the password." I crossed my fingers, but as soon as I heard the fork clink against his plate, I knew he wouldn't give it up.

"Coming."

I did my best to watch as he entered it. Unfortunately, his sausage fingers flew across the keyboard in such rapid succession I caught nothing.

"There you go," he said and walked off.

With that, I finally had some answers.

Ushabti: a stone figurine commonplace among ancient Egyptian funerary practice.

I scratched my head. If King Tut confused me for a stone figurine, he must have died from a head injury. I read on for clarification.

These figurines were placed within a tomb alongside food and whatever else the individual needed in the afterlife. Egyptians believed the Ushabti would function as a servant for the deceased.

I skimmed the rest of the page, but it didn't give me much else to work with. In summary, my fart planned to enslave me for manual labor.

Cleaning bathrooms suddenly didn't sound so bad.

I clicked on the search bar and moved onto my next search.

How to break a curse.

Results filled the screen. I clicked on the first link (that's where you find the most popular one, right?).

It read like a potion recipe. Now we were talking. I grabbed a scrap piece of paper and a pencil from the desk caddy and jotted down the ingredients.

Water for a base. Add lemon for taste.

For protection, 2 parts salt and 1 ground basalt.

3 hummingbird wings...

Hummingbird wings?

I skipped ahead. The list grew increasingly ridiculous with each new line. A dragon's horn. Hairs from a unicorn.

If ghosts existed, dragons and unicorns might, too. But the rhyming thing seemed awfully suspicious.

I checked the top of the page.

Ugh. This was an entry for a poetry contest.

Maybe I needed to be more specific.

How to break an ancient Egyptian curse.

This produced a brand-new list of links. First, a Wikipedia article on the curse of the Pharaohs. Curses 'weren't real.' Our museum guide had covered all that. I moved on.

'The Process of Cursing in Ancient Egypt.'

My eyes lit up. If I knew how they crafted curses, maybe I could reverse engineer it. Then I spotted the note at the bottom. Three hundred and twenty-nine pages.

Great... If I could read sixty pages a minute.

If the internet had no suggestions on breaking the curse, I'd have to try something else. I tapped the table while I thought.

Aha. No farting meant no King Toot. My fingers hen-pecked another question.

How do I stop farting?

Farting is a natural step in the digestive process. When bacteria in the gut breaks down food, gas becomes a natural byproduct.

A normal person farts anywhere between ten and twenty times a day. However, certain hard to digest foods like beans or raw vegetables may cause more gas.

More bad news. First, I couldn't stop myself from farting. Second, I didn't fit the classification of 'normal people' any longer. Normal people weren't cursed by Egyptian ghosts. Ten or twenty was a vast understatement.

And Mom made sure I ate my vegetables. Time for another pivot.

Foods that cause stinky farts.

Foods naturally high in fiber or sulfur can produce more gas, and flatulence that smells worse...

"Mom!" Leyla yelled. "John's not doing homework. He's been sitting here Googling farts for the last twenty minutes."

I clicked on the little 'X' in the corner and opened Microsoft Word, but it was far too late.

Mom stormed into the family room and delivered a death glare. "Dishes. Now."

I stood. "But I haven't even started my homework."

Okay. **THAT** was the wrong thing to say.

"You mean the homework you left the table early to work on? What have you been doing?"

"I told you," Leyla said. "He's been looking up fart facts. Check the browser history."

"Umm..." I made a mental note to prepare a better excuse ahead of time. "I got distracted."

"I don't think he even has homework..."

"I'll handle this," Mom said, turning to my sister. "If you still want to talk to your friends, you'll butt your way out."

Leyla didn't need to be told twice. She waited till Mom wasn't paying attention, stuck her tongue out, and squeezed past me into the computer chair.

"I DO have homework, Mom. I swear. I have to report on what I learned during the museum trip."

"Perfect. You can work from memory and not the computer. When I was your age, we prepared our speeches on index cards. There's a whole mess of them in one of the boxes inside your room.

"When you're done loading the dishwasher, I suggest you start unpacking your room and find them."

"But..."

"No buts, young man."

I sulked back into the kitchen and moved dishes from the table to the counter.

Meanwhile, Mom retired to the couch with her book, and Dad started packing up the leftovers. On my last trip, he walked up beside me and held his hand out.

"Pull my finger."

I ignored him and turned on the faucet.

"Oof," he said. "Not even a smile.

"Here." He took the plate from my hands and rinsed the bulk of the enchilada sauce and congealed cheese into the sink. He handed it off to me and I slotted it into the dishwasher. "I'll tag-team it with you."

"Thanks," I said.

"We all have bad days. Can I give you some advice?"

I looked up at him. "What?"

"I have bad days, too. It's part of life. But you can make sure it doesn't ruin your entire week. When you find a day that can't be salvaged, go to sleep and hope the next day is better. That's what I do."

He handed over the final plate. "Tomorrow will be a better day. I can feel it."

No part of me believed that, but I faked a smile anyway. "Thanks, Dad."

I grabbed my bookbag and trudged up to my room. The clock read six fifteen on the dot. It had been three hours since I'd last farted. It wouldn't be long now.

I needed protection.

Mom always complained about how much time Dad spent in their bathroom. Not to mention how much he stunk up the place. I'd find air freshener in there.

Since they were both downstairs, I wouldn't need to answer any questions. Thirty seconds later, I had myself a can of 'Linen & Sky'-scented Toot repellant.

My stomach rumbled. Hunger pains, nothing else. Lunch was six hours ago, and I was already starving. Not eating wasn't an option.

At best, I could find something to take my mind off things. I didn't have much other than moving boxes. Sure, there were things *inside* the moving boxes, but that required work.

Maybe Dad was right. I took a seat on the edge of the bed and checked the clock. It wasn't even six thirty, but the mattress already had a firm hold on me. At some point, I leaned back and rested my eyes.

The next thing I knew, Dad's voice was shouting through my door.

"Get up John. You don't want to be late for the first day of school."

First day of school?

My eyes opened, and I sat up from the most restful night of sleep in my existence. I scanned the bed.

There was no bottle of air freshener.

My hands shot to my stomach. No terrible aching and no gas bubbles. There was no pain in my belly, unless you counted that 'woke up hungry' sensation. I fell back onto my pillow.

I blew out a deep breath. The pyramids, the sand, King Tut shoving me into a sarcophagus—it was just a stupid nightmare. Curses didn't exist. I yawned and rolled onto my side.

"Five more minutes."

"You don't want to miss the bus." Dad pounded on my door, and my eyes snapped open again.

King Toot's translucent form stood in the corner of my room. A smile crept across his bronzed face.

"You fart in your sleep."

CHAPTER 13
SAVED BY THE BELL

I screamed and backed away from the ghost. Note: this is easier said than done while on a raised platform. I ran out of real estate, hit my back on the corner of the nightstand, and tumbled to the floor. The entire nightstand came after me. My arm went up and kept the furniture from falling on top of me. Or at least most of it.

The drawer flew out, and the pull handle cracked me in the middle of my head. On the plus side, I spotted the blue and white aluminum can under my bed.

I grabbed the air freshener and hopped to my feet. King Toot kept his distance. He raised his royal scepter.

"Ushabti..."

"Are you okay?" Dad called.

"Yeah, yeah. I know," I said, holding out the can. "You think I'm your Ushabti."

My hand shook as I stepped around my bed. I wasn't sure exactly how far this thing could reach.

Stall until you get closer.

"I'm sorry I ate your cheese. It was an accident. I'm just a kid like you."

King Toot opened his mouth, but the doorknob turned before he could speak. He darted aside.

Dad was faster.

The door swung through the ghost, dissipating his midsection and tail.

"Who are you talking to?" Dad asked, looking around.

I dropped the air freshener and kicked it back under my bed.

"Uhh... Nobody."

"Man, John. It smells like a toilet in here." Dad waved his hand in front of his nose.

The remainder of King Toot distorted into long, wispy threads as Dad rushed across my room. I swore I heard him wail something as he got sucked out the open window.

"Maybe it's a good thing you skipped the enchiladas." He leaned closer and reduced his voice to a whisper. "You didn't poop your bed, did you?"

My face turned red. "No."

"It happens. If you're sick, you can stay home from school."

In hindsight, I would have pooped my bed yesterday to stay home. But right now, I needed my friends. They were the only ones who understood what I was going through. That meant going to school.

"I feel fine. I'm looking forward to meeting the rest of my classmates. Besides, it's Friday."

Dad retreated to the hallway. He returned a moment later to add, "Make sure you change your underwear."

"Okay, Dad." I closed my door and admitted to myself he was right. I'd gone nose blind to all the overnight farting. A fresh pair of clothes did wonders and, all things considered, I didn't *feel* cursed.

Maybe the apology had worked.

In fact, the rest of the morning went pretty smoothly. My new friends weren't on my bus route, but neither was Butt-crack Steve. When I got to school, I found Other John, Akira, and Park waiting for me outside.

I waved at them as I got off the bus. All three smiled back.

"We weren't sure if you were going to show up," Other John said.

He stuck out his hand as I approached. I went for a high five, but instead, he pressed something into my palm.

"What's this?"

I looked down after he pulled his hand back. It was one of those green, Christmas tree-shaped air fresheners.

The group headed inside the building, so I followed.

"Something that's been sitting unused in my dad's truck for the last six months. I thought it might help. That is... if you still have a problem?"

"Yup." I unwrapped the little tree and stuffed it in my back pocket. "He was waiting in my room this morning."

I stopped in the middle of the hallway. Did I imagine it, or did King Toot speak English?

Other John turned around. "What is it?"

"He spoke English. I mean... he called me Ushabti again, but he also told me I farted in my sleep. That part was in English."

Park and Other John giggled.

"You think he spent all night learning our language?" Park asked.

Akira shook her head. "If it's really King Tut's ghost, he's been hanging in the spirit realm for thousands of years. English isn't that complicated." She pointed to her brother and Other John. "I mean, they figured it out."

"Real funny," said Park. "You should ask Mom which one of us spoke first." He turned back to me. "Did he say anything other than the sleep-farting thing?"

"No." I shrugged. "He was about to, but my dad sorta slammed my bedroom door through him."

A bell rang, and kids hurried their way through the corridors.

"Come on. Mrs. Barwick's classroom is this way," Akira said.

"And she hates it when you're tardy," her brother added.

I sat through a few boring hours of school but won't make you do the same. I'll recap as quickly as possible for your sake.

Mrs. Barwick allowed us to pick our own seats, which was super cool. I chose the one closest to the window for obvious reasons. Other John took the desk beside me, Akira in front, and Park diagonal.

Butt-crack Steve tried to sit behind me, but another student beat him to it. That was also super cool. The coolest thing, though, was that everyone in the class got a school-issued laptop. And we got to bring it home. No more sharing a family computer with my sister.

Between getting everyone settled with their computers and getting our names on our folders and whatnot, there wasn't much time for anything else. Then it was off to lunch. An individual pepperoni pizza (which was surprisingly better than my last school).

From lunch it was straight to recess.

That concludes our recap. This is the part you've been waiting for: the next fart.

Apology or not, my intestines had produced more curse gas. But hey, at least the terrible cramps were gone.

Of all the places to let out an earth-shattering, nose-melting bottom burp, the playground was ideal.

I whipped around at the first hint of rotten eggs and pine.

The midday sun cast King Toot in a golden glow as he rose to full height. Under other circumstances, it would have made for a great magazine cover. He was downright majestic, at least for a fart.

Other John pinched his nose and fumbled for the air freshener.

"No!" I jumped in front of him. "Running hasn't solved the problem."

I faced the Egyptian ruler and cleared my throat. Here goes nothing.

"Excuse me, Mr. Toot."

The ghost's head zipped within inches of my face.

I glanced back nervously at my friends, hoping they'd save my butt if anything bad happened.

"Err... I'm sorry we keep getting interrupted, Mr. Tutankhamun. Can you kindly tell me what you want from me?"

His lips parted.

My heart pounded. I was finally about to hear his demands.

"Head's up, Fartstink."

I turned my head just as a kickball passed through the back of King Tut's head, emerged out the front, and clobbered me between the eyes. My glasses went flying and skidded across the blacktop.

"Oops."

Butt-crack Steve doubled over laughing.

I bent over and snagged my glasses. They were bent out of shape, but some light pressure got them even. Mostly.

My face burned. It wasn't enough that this kid had broken my zipper, eaten my Oreos, and gotten me this stupid curse. Now, he'd interrupted *another* chance to get to the bottom of it.

I spun on my heels and stared him down.

"Watch it, Butt-crack Steve!"

All around the schoolyard kickballs hit the ground and bounced away from their owners. Children gasped and stared. Nobody said a word.

Stephen rolled up his sleeves and marched toward me.

"What. Did. You. Say?"

Akira spoke without moving her lips. "The last kid who said that to his face got his nose broken."

I gulped.

The bell rang, and Mrs. Barwick headed toward our group. I was never so happy to see a teacher in my entire life.

"Hurry, Mr. Pahrsink. The class is anxiously awaiting your presentation."

Oh... That.

CHAPTER 14

THE PORCELAIN THRONE OF EGYPT

I stood in front of twenty-some pairs of eyes watching my every move. I didn't deserve this. Nobody did.

"Since some of you couldn't attend yesterday's field trip, John volunteered to give a brief report on the Egyptian wing."

Mrs. Barwick motioned toward me.

"Please give him your attention."

"The exhibit on ancient Egypt was pretty awesome." I glanced over at the teacher. She didn't seem particularly amused, but I literally remembered nothing from the trip thanks to Butt-crack Steve. As my eyes picked him out of the crowd, he held up his pencil and snapped it in half.

I reached up and touched the bridge of my nose. In his early twenties, my Uncle Stan had broken his nose playing hockey. It was crooked the rest of his life.

Mrs. Barwick looked on, expecting more. I fiddled with my belt loops and tried to remember something else. Anything else.

"Oh. You enter the exhibit through a giant Mu..." *Uh-oh, what was the word our guide used?* "Mufasa."

I knew it was the wrong word as soon as it came out, but the damage was done. My face grew redder as a few students giggled.

"Shhh..." Mrs. Barwick said. The class actually listened, even if some still snickered to themselves. "Please continue."

A loud foghorn of a fart caught me off guard. Heck, it caught everyone off guard. I didn't even realize it came from me until the smell hit.

There was a chorus of laughter, groans, and disgust.

"Okay, class. Let's be mature." Mrs. Barwick said. Her nose crinkled up, and she coughed a little. "It's completely natural," she added as she rushed over and cracked a window.

Other John jumped up and pointed behind me. Unfortunately, I was too busy burying my face in my hands to notice.

"John! What do you think you're doing?"

"I'm sorry, my stomach…"

"Not you, the other John."

Akira and Park snickered.

"Sit down so your classmate can continue his presentation." She turned to me. "Unless you need to be excused to the restroom."

Mrs. Barwick screwed up her face again. "Or the nurse's office."

The class snickered again.

As much as I had something to prove, this was a perfect opportunity. I could feel King Toot's presence behind me, watching.

"I'm sorry," I said. "I should—"

"Mastaba," King Toot said with a sigh. "It has nothing to do with a cartoon lion. It's Arabic for bench."

Wait a minute. How did King Tut know about The Lion King?

Mrs. Barwick raised an eyebrow. "Yes?"

"Uh…" I cleared my throat. "The entrance to the Egyptian wing is a Mastaba, which is Arabic for bench."

Okay. If Tut feeds me all the answers, I'm set. I'll get Mrs. Barwick off my back and sort out the ghost stuff later.

He had other ideas.

King Toot swooped around in front of me. His face solidified, blotting out my classmates. I crossed my fingers, waiting for Other John to rescue me. Except I'd called him off earlier. And presumably, he couldn't see the fear on my face either.

"*You* are no Ushabti..." The ghost's voice came out harsh and grating. "You defiled my belongings."

"I'm sorry," I whispered. "I didn't mean to eat your cheese. I'll be your Ushabti."

"Please speak up," Mrs. Barwick said. "We can't hear you."

The ghost inched closer.

I clamped my eyes shut and held my breath. There's no way I'd get to the tree in my pocket in time. I was going back to ancient Egypt any second now.

"John?" said Mrs. Barwick.

I couldn't stand here all day and hide behind my eyelids. One of my eyes popped open, then the other.

Tut was back to his original, transparent self. More importantly, he was no longer directly in my face.

"Sorry," I repeated.

My ghost bowed and I sensed we had a truce. Though I still wasn't sure what that meant for me.

"Mastaba were smaller tombs," I said, my voice a little shaky. "They were flat and rectangular, not like the pyramids. These marked the burials of important individuals, but not as prolific as, say, King Tutankhamun."

The words flowed from my mouth without conscious thought. Maybe I knew more than I thought. Or maybe it was a telepathic info-dump directly from ol' Tutty himself. Whatever the source, the facts kept coming.

"Death didn't mark the end in ancient Egyptian culture. In fact, the afterlife was even more important. They buried their dead with anything they needed in the afterlife: clothing, food, and, in the case of the royal class, servants."

I paused to take a breath and Mrs. Barwick stepped forward. "Thank you, John."

Other John began clapping, which spread to Akira, Park, and eventually the rest of the class (except for Butt-crack Steve, of course).

Our teacher stared at me for a moment. "I don't recall most of those facts from our tour."

I gulped.

"But since you were under the weather, I'm impressed you researched on your own. You may take your seat."

King Toot floated alongside me as I started my way back to my desk. When I stopped and turned around, he did as well.

"Actually, I'd like to use the restroom, if that's okay."

She nodded and nearly threw the bathroom pass at me. I grabbed the blue piece of plywood shaped like a person and headed into the hallway.

I ducked into the first stall of the boy's room, locked the door behind me, and perched on the edge of the toilet.

"Okay," I said. "How does this work?"

King Toot looked around. "This is no place for a king."

Before I could explain that it was the most private place we'd get, Toot raised his hand. The quite solid-looking bejeweled scepter appeared from thin air, which he gently tapped to my forehead.

The bathroom lurched sideways, taking my stomach with it. When I opened my eyes (and stopped screaming), we were somewhere else. And probably sometime else.

King Tut looked down on me from a towering golden throne. "Much better."

He wasn't wrong. The bathroom had transformed into a palace before my very eyes. Orange metal stall walls had become sandstone bricks engraved with hieroglyphics. Metal enclosures with roaring fires stood in for the fluorescent bulbs. Though I looked around for a comparison to the urinal pucks, I came up empty.

I touched the closest flame. It hurt. A lot. The sandstone around it felt rough to the touch as well.

Tut watched patiently as I explored the rest of the space. The room was huge, significantly larger than the stall I'd left behind. Plus, it smelled sweet and was nothing like an elementary school bathroom.

Trying to figure out this ghost magic hurt my brain, so I turned back toward my host. There was nothing translucent about him. And he was every bit as grand as his surroundings.

I looked down at my T-shirt, jean shorts, and sneakers. He had crisp white robes with gold trim, a golden headdress, gold rings, and winged staff (made of gold, of course).

My hair was... kind of golden?

Dread filled my stomach. This man was royalty and I locked him in the crapper.

"I apologize," I said, kneeling in front of him. "My king."

Ugh. Super cringe.

Why did I add that last part? Of course, he wasn't *MY* king. And he knew that.

"I mean... Mr. Tutankhamun? What should I call you?"

"Rise."

I did as he asked.

He leaned forward and rested his weight against the staff. "Explain yourself."

"Well, you see, your kingship." I winced. "I was at the museum, which apparently had one of your artifacts. A vase.

"Butt-crack Steve shoved me and knocked over your vase. Your cheese fell out and mistakenly wound up in my lunch bag..." The rest came out in a whisper. "And I sort of ate it.

"Now here I am. Cursed." It took conscious effort to skip 'to fart you out,' but I managed.

King Tut stroked his chin.

"Very well. I shall lift the curse."

I almost fell forward and kissed his sandals.

"On one condition."

"Of course," I said. "Name it."

"You will help recover all my stolen possessions."

I blinked. "What?"

"Thieves plundered my tomb. You, Ushabti, will return what was destined for me in the afterlife."

"But I'm *not* Ushabti. And your items were stolen thousands of years ago. They're either long gone, held by private collectors, or are stuck in museums all over the world."

"And?"

"I don't have a driver's license or a passport. I'm just a kid." I gestured toward the ghost. "Like you."

"I am the pharaoh of the eighteenth dynasty of Egypt. I am not a child."

Tut was right. People back then probably only lived until their forties. He was technically middle-aged.

"I meant no offense. It's not that I don't want to help you, it's just impossible for me to do those things."

He continued staring at me, and I realized he still didn't understand. I thought back to the articles I'd read last night. Maybe I could pull this off.

"Your tomb contained everything you needed in the afterlife. Food, furs, treasure. It's been thousands of years. Most of the food and fabric are probably dust by now. They're unrecoverable."

"Hmm..." More chin stroking. "You are wise."

I wasn't sure whether that was a good thing, especially since he wanted something from me, but I thanked him anyway.

"Then you shall replace those perishable goods with new items."

"Yes," I said with a nod. That was a start. But maybe I could do better.

"Do you realize you've been in the afterlife for centuries? You've been okay without all those things this far."

A terrible rumble shook the palace. The fires flared, warming my skin. Sand and dust fell from the walls. For a moment, I feared the wrath of the gods. But the disembodied voice I heard next was no Egyptian deity.

"I knew you were gross, Fartstink, but talking to your turds? That's a new level of weird."

The palace, including King Tut, faded away, and I was back in the school bathroom. With a bully. Who, according to Akira, had planned on breaking my nose.

"Quit hiding in the toilet."

The stall doors rattled beneath what I can only assume was the bully's meaty fist.

"I'm a little busy."

"Pinch it off. We have something to discuss."

"Umm... one minute."

I looked around. There were two ways out: beneath the stall walls, or out through the door. Neither was a great choice. Stephen was bigger and would catch me no matter what. Going out the door at least gave me a chance. And maintained my dignity, I guess.

The door creaked open.

Stephen cracked his knuckles.

"*Nobody* calls me Butt-crack Steve. Here's a reminder so you won't forget."

His fist zipped toward my face.

I ducked past him, and his momentum carried him into the stall.

There was a flash of motion in the mirror.

Stephen grumbled something unintelligible.

Wait... Nope.

That was ancient Egyptian.

King Toot darted *into* my attacker.

Stephen stumbled backward and the stall door slammed shut.

I turned to run, then froze. On the one hand, Stephen wanted to pummel me into next week. But on the other hand, he was alone with the ghost who'd cursed me. Bully or not, I had to help him.

"Stephen?" I called. "Are you okay?"

I really should have run.

There was another sound. Not Egyptian. Not even English.

Just '*Hurk!*'

It was like someone had opened a fire hydrant inside the stall. Well, if the hydrant connected straight to the city's puke pipes, anyway.

Green vomit rained from the heavens.

CHAPTER 15
TOOT'S LAST TOOT

Believe it or not, there are a couple of upsides to being coated in vomit. You get out of school and your family has to be super nice to you. Vomapocalypse even got me out of cleaning my room.

So when the doorbell rang, I kept right on playing video games from the couch and drinking my giant cherry Slurpee.

"John," Mom called. "You have visitors."

I hit pause and tossed the controller on the couch.

"Come on in," Mom said as I rounded the corner.

My new friends stood together in our entryway. Park had my bookbag in his hand.

"Oh, hey, guys," I said. "Thanks for bringing my backpack over."

I turned to Mom and smiled. "Thanks. I've got it from here."

My friends looked at one another and waited till she walked off.

"Uh... What happened to you?" Other John asked.

"Yeah," Akira said. "There were all kinds of crazy rumors going around the school."

As usual, Park chimed in immediately after his sister. "Adrian said the bathroom was full of blood. But Peter said it was just diarrhea and vomit. One of the fourth graders said you left in an ambulance."

"Does it look like I went to the hospital?"

They all shook their heads.

"So what did happen?" Other John leaned forward, ready for confirmation.

"I had a long talk with King Toot. He promised he'd remove the curse. But not until *after* I return all his stolen artifacts. Or at least replace them with something similar."

"I don't care about that. Did you kick Steve's butt, or what?"

"I explained to King Tut how this whole thing was Steve's fault, and he got justice." I shrugged. "Or protected me. I'm not sure which."

"But what exactly happened to him?" Other John pleaded.

"Toot turned him into a human puke fountain. I slipped on my way out of the bathroom and hit my head."

"Ouch," Akira said. "At least you got to go home early."

"And get a Slurpee," added Park.

"I spent thirty minutes washing chunks out of my hair."

I sighed. "But it's okay. It gave me time to plan King Toot's demise."

Other John threw his hands in the air.

"You've got a superpower. Why would you want to get rid of a ghost who can help with all your history homework?"

Park punched the air in front of him (and almost took off his sister's head on the backswing). "And make your enemies soil themselves!"

"Boys," Akira said with a shake of her head. "Ushabti were servants. John is basically King Toot's property."

"Not to mention I stink!" I added. "Should we ask King Toot to transfer the curse to one of you?"

Everyone shook their heads.

"Got it," Other John said. "Stinky farts are bad. What's your plan?"

I held my hands out. "I'm going to ask my parents to bring me back to the museum this weekend and leave a Babybel in the vase to replace the one I ate."

Nobody looked impressed.

"Yeah," Akira said. "That's a terrible idea. Do you think cheap, mass-produced cheese is gonna' impress the ghost of Egypt's most famous pharaoh?"

I blinked. Well, I had up till now.

"I have a better idea." She pulled out a notebook and jotted something down. "Do you think your mom will let you come back to the museum with us tomorrow?"

"Yeah. Probably."

Akira ripped the corner off and handed over the scrap of paper. "Here's my dad's number. He wouldn't stop talking about how he hasn't been back to the museum since he was a boy. I'm sure we can convince him to take the three of us back there tomorrow."

Other John grinned. "And me too, right?"

Akira sighed. "Fine. The four of us."

She grabbed her brother's arm and pulled him out the door.

"Wait," I called after them. "What's the plan?"

"I've got it covered. Trust me."

The rest of the day was quiet, Toot wise. If you must know, I did fart a few times. None of them were heinous enough to summon you-know-who.

By Saturday afternoon, I felt great. Optimistic, even. I trusted Akira. She had proven herself to be the brains of the group. For example, it was a great idea to go along with her dad. He let us go into the mastaba by ourselves as long as we met him upstairs by the T-Rex afterward. Mom and Dad would have never left us unattended.

The four of us huddled together over the plexiglass square that looked down into the sarcophagus room below.

I bounced on the balls of my feet. "Can you finally tell me your plan?"

Akira pulled a bundle of paper from her bag and passed it to me.

"You're making an official offering to the former king of Egypt."

I took the funny feeling envelope in my hands and turned it.

She grabbed my wrist and kept it level. "Be careful. It's full of saffron."

"Saffron?"

"An exotic spice," Park said.

"Not just an exotic spice," corrected Akira. "It's the world's most *expensive* spice. A fitting tribute for royalty."

"That sounds great."

"When we get downstairs, sign your name inside. Then we'll slip it inside the vase."

We retraced our footsteps from Wednesday and wound through the ancient Egypt exhibit, right up to the vase in question.

"Okay," Akira said. "Open the paper and sign your name at the bottom."

I found where the outermost fold of paper had been tucked around the rest and tugged.

A red thread floated to the ground. That was the so-called world's most expensive spice?

"Careful!"

"Okay, okay." I moved the bundle to a nearby table and spread it open. Tufts of clumped red fuzz obscured the most elaborate but illegible handwriting I'd ever seen.

"This is your expensive spice?"

"Yes," Akira said. "Here. Your turn." She handed me a metal-tipped pen.

"But my handwriting won't match yours."

"It's Grandma's. She's the calligraphy buff. But it shouldn't matter. It's the gesture that counts."

"Okay. Here goes."

Without much cursive practice, my signature looked more like John Fartstink than I was comfortable with. As I tried to re-fold the corners, I ended up leaving a little smear.

I gently blew on the fresh ink. Threads of saffron swirled around on the paper.

"Careful!" Akira said again. She folded up the edges and placed it back in my hands.

My heart beat faster. I was one step closer to ending the curse. All that remained was putting this fancy apology into the urn.

"Okay, give me a hand with the case, guys."

I kept a lookout as Other John and Park placed their hands around the glass enclosure.

"Uh. Problem, boss," Other John said. "They repaired the loose case."

I dropped to my knees and inspected the freshly caulked seams. Short of breaking the seal, we weren't getting inside.

"Great. Just perfect." I turned to Akira. She seemed to have all the answers. "Now what?"

"I don't know… Fart and hand it to King Toot himself?"

My ghost hadn't shown himself in twenty-four hours, but it was worth a shot. I closed my eyes and pushed.

Akira, Other John, and Park all stepped out of smelling distance.

Pushing with all my might didn't help. Neither did squatting or lifting one leg.

"It's not working. I can't just fart on command."

I looked around. There were a lot of other cases. Maybe one of them was loose. Though, we had no guarantees that anything else in the exhibit was a former possession of Tutankhamun.

Where did that leave us? Hope that one of the museum curators believed my story and let me inside the case? Head to the cafeteria and scarf down a bunch of beans? Maybe we could leave it under the urn. I set the package on the floor. One edge slipped beneath the base of the pedestal.

"Uhh…" I cleared my throat. "Ushabti here. I give you this offering to replace all that's been taken from you."

I shoved the rest of the paper under the pedestal, ensuring nobody would take it. Then I bowed and got to my feet.

My friends stared at me, and one by one, joined my side.

"That's it?" Other John said.

"Maybe?" I said with a shrug.

I wasn't expecting a blinding flash of light or anything, but I did expect to feel... I don't know. Something.

Come to think of it, I hadn't gotten a whiff of Toot since he attacked Butt-crack Steve (and I'd farted plenty since).

That thought stuck with me through the rest of our museum visit, the ride home, and even following dinner with my family.

If King Toot wasn't hanging out in my farts, where was he? Was he still in Stephen?

I dug through my backpack and found the class directory they passed out on our first day of school. While I never caught Butt-crack Steve's last name, there was only one entry in our grade for a Stephen with a P.H. Stephen Stern.

There was a corresponding phone number listed for Jessica Stern. With that number in hand, I found my mom in the living room on her favorite reading chair.

"Can I borrow your phone so I can make a call?"

She lowered her book and looked me up and down. "It's getting close to bedtime."

"I want to call the kid who got sick yesterday and see how he's feeling."

"Oh." She grabbed her phone off the glass table beside her and punched in her lock code. "That's sweet."

She held it out but pulled it back as soon as I reached for it.

"Promise you'll bring it back right after the call."

I nodded. "Promise."

I ran up the stairs to my room and shut my door.

After a few rings, Stephen's mom answered.

"Hi, Mrs. Stern. I'm one of Stephen's classmates. Can I speak with him, please?"

"Sure. One moment." The line fell quiet for a moment and then she yelled out her son's name.

"Uh... Hello?" His voice was kinder than I'd anticipated. I guessed he hadn't expected I'd call.

"Bu—" I slapped my forehead. *Can't believe I almost called him that again.* "Stephen?"

"Fartstink." There was the anger I expected in his voice. "What do *you* want?"

"Yesterday was crazy, huh?"

Really, that's the first thing my mind went to?

"What do you want?"

"Apparently, there are a lot of rumors going around school. I wanted to see if you were okay."

He paused. "What do you care?"

"It was just pretty crazy."

"Yeah," Stephen said. "You said that already."

"Are you still feeling sick?"

"No."

"So, you're not still vomiting? Or you know, farting a lot? Or seeing things?"

"I see myself hanging up."

Neither of us said anything for a good minute.

I broke the silence. "You seemed really sick. I just wanted to make sure you were okay."

Stephen grunted. "Just so we're clear, calling to check up on me doesn't make us friends, Fartstink."

Before I could say anything else, he hung up.

I sat on the edge of my bed and stared at Mom's phone. My reasons for calling Stephen were mostly selfish. I wanted confirmation that he'd taken the curse off my hands.

Still, there was a tiny part of me hoping the incident would instill some empathy into him. That was too much to hope for.

Bzzzt.

I jumped as Mom's phone vibrated in my hand. The number on the display was one I knew well. Mom's sister. Kooky Aunt Lucille.

My finger hit the answer button without thinking.

"John," Aunt Lucille said, interrupting my 'Hello.' "You're in grave danger."

CHAPTER 16
A FAMILY OF FARTERS

I rolled my eyes. If everyone in my family had a dollar every time Aunt Lucille called with a dire warning, we'd be rich.

You don't know my aunt, but this will give you an idea. She believes in horoscopes and that the numbers at the bottom of fortune cookies really are lucky. Not that I didn't like her. She was great, especially if you liked getting shiny rocks every time she visited.

"My spirit guides told me you need help. I'll be there as soon as I find someone to watch your cousins for a few days."

Ah yes. My 'cousins.'

Aunt Lucille didn't have any kids. She meant her insane number of cats. Though, if you ask me, any number of cats is too many.

I could never keep track of how many cats Aunt Lucille had at any given time. She was constantly bringing in strays, fostering shelter cats, or losing ones she'd owned for ages.

Sorry, I'm getting off topic. The important part is that Aunt Lucille thinks she's psychic. Which is odd, since she spends hundreds of dollars a month on psychic readings. Real plumbers don't pay someone else to fix their own pipes.

"Something bad already happened. I can feel it."

If any adult would understand, it would be Aunt Lucille. Even so, I couldn't bring myself to tell her.

"You're scaring me," she said. "Why are you so quiet?"

"I'm..."

The words still wouldn't come out.

"It can be our little secret. I promise."

"I'm..."

Butterflies flitted around my stomach.

"Yes?"

I shut my eyes so tight they hurt. "Cursed."

"Cursed," my aunt repeated half a second after me.

Okay... that was weird, but it was just a coincidence. She copied what I said. There's no way she could have guessed that part.

"Yes. I understand now. It's ancient. Sumerian, maybe? No. Wait. Egyptian."

My eyes snapped back open, and the blood in my veins went ice cold.

We'd poked fun at Aunt Lucille for her crystals and stuff for years. Did she really know about this stuff?

"We'll sort this out. Don't worry."

I wanted her to be wrong. The alternative meant I hadn't beaten the curse on my own. But at the same time, I welcomed an expert's help.

"I'm worried. I don't know what to do."

"I will be there as soon as I can. Put your mom on the phone and we'll work out the details."

"Okay. Let me get her."

I hurried, practically falling down the stairs, and held out the phone to my mother.

"Aunt Lucille."

"Thanks," Mom said, putting the phone to her ear.

I stood there while they exchanged pleasantries. Would she tell Mom about my curse?

No. She'd promised.

But what exactly was she saying? Mom watched me watching her, and I realized how suspicious the whole thing looked.

By then I'd been standing there so long I had to say something.

"I'm going to go upstairs and read."

Mom waved me away.

I stopped at the pantry on the way upstairs and fished around in the giant box of granola bars. Nope. Peanut butter. I wasn't allergic, I just didn't particularly like the flavor. I dug back in and tried again.

Chocolate chip. Okay, but I could do better.

Ugh. Peanut butter again.

After one more try, I hit the jackpot. S'mores.

Mom didn't like us eating outside the kitchen. But if I stuffed the wrapper in the bathroom trash, she'd never know.

I scarfed down the granola bar, found the box with all my graphic novels, and took one to my bed. After twenty-five minutes, I hadn't made it past the first page.

My mind kept replaying the last two days. The museum. Butt-crack Steve. Aunt Lucille. I groaned and rolled onto my side where my alarm clock was in full view.

Eight-fifteen.

Even if Akira's plan didn't work, I had this under control. It had now been well over thirty hours since I last tooted Toot. That was when a new revelation hit me. I hadn't eaten any cheese since Thursday.

Cutting cheese out of my diet wouldn't be terrible. I've heard a lot of people become lactose intolerant later in life anyway. Not like I could look at another Babybel.

And if King Toot reared his stinky head even after going cheese-free, I'd deal with it. I knew what he wanted. He might even enjoy one of Aunt Lucille's crystals.

A lot of good things had happened to me in the past two days. I wasn't alone. I had great new friends willing to put up with my gas. Plus, I no longer had to share the family computer with Leyla thanks to my school laptop (and, after begging, she taught me how to clear the browser history).

This curse might change my life drastically, but it wouldn't bring it to an end. I could still play video games and hang out with my friends.

I picked the book back up. When I finished with that one, I grabbed the sequel, and then the third in the series.

I read until someone knocked on my bedroom door.

"Come in," I said, looking up from the book.

Dad leaned in from the hallway. "It's ten-thirty, buddy. Lights out, okay?"

"I'm in the middle of this chapter. Five more minutes?"

"Okay," he said. "Fifteen minutes max."

I nodded. He shut the door behind him.

Life felt normal again. So I'm sure you know what happened next. I got a little too relaxed.

As I finished that chapter, a small gas bubble built up in my stomach. I didn't think twice before letting it rip.

The smell sprang me out of bed like the ejector seat of a fighter jet.

King Toot returned, right on cue. Only this time, he wasn't alone.

I did a double take as a second gaseous form... Well, formed.

Beside Toot stood an older gentleman with curly, white hair I was certain was a wig. His dress was nothing like the Egyptian ruler's.

There was something familiar about the man that I couldn't put my finger on. I'd seen the black hat, overcoat, and white scarf recently. Someone from the museum displays?

No. I didn't think so.

There was one way to find out.

I looked at King Toot and pointed at the old-timey ghost. "Who the heck is that?"

King Toot shrugged.

"My name is Larry, lad." The unidentified man straightened out the wrinkles in his jacket and looked around my room. "Now... Where might I be?"

I looked down at the granola bar wrapper lying on my bed and then back up to my newest ghost.

You've got to be kidding me.

I'd just farted out the Quaker Oatmeal guy.

AFTERWORD
THE END?

That concludes my "origin" story, but things are far(t) from over.

No happy ending for me. As of the time of writing this book, I'm still cursed. I do hope you read on, though. Because let me tell you... farting out the Quaker Oatmeal mascot was the tip of the iceberg.

Acknowledgments
(From the actual author)

Writing a book is not easy. The dedication I chose for this book is funny, but it's not fair to leave the real heroes uncredited. Especially my family.

The idea behind John's Fart-Ripping Adventures came one night while my son, Nate, sat in bed reading Captain Underpants.

I joked about combining a similar style of potty humor with some brief history lessons and maybe a few vocabulary lessons as well. The idea of a kid who farts out historical ghosts was born.

My son LOVED the idea and begged me to write it. My wife too urged me to make it a reality before he grew out of fart jokes (as if anyone can be too old for fart jokes). Thus, JFRA was born.

Once the book was nearly complete, I knew it needed a little something extra. I asked Nate to lend a hand with interior illustrations. He is a stellar artist, and it's been amazing to watch his skills progress over the years. He definitely nailed the style of the cover (more on that later).

Zach, my nephew, deserves a share of inspirational credit as well. We were discussing the ideas behind JFRA, and out of nowhere he shouted, "You should make a character named Butt-crack Steve." Without hesitation, I said 'Okay.' I knew I needed a bully character, and BS was perfect.

Now, onto the cover. I also write urban fantasy books for adults (tell your parents to buy them). I've been selling books alongside the Streetz Arts Alliance—a group packed full of amazing artists. I knew Jon Belonio was the man for the job.

I commissioned a cover from him before I even started writing. Boy, was that the right choice. Jon's illustration provided the perfect motivation to make this story a reality.

You should check out Belonio Doodles when you have a chance. Our house is chock full of his art.

And that's not all. I am blessed enough to have a LOT of author friends. Marty, Krista, and Britta all provided much needed encouragement, cover design tips, and not to mention Krista's proofreading.

There's a moral to this long-winded acknowledgment. Never be afraid to ask for help. We wouldn't have a society without teamwork.

This is Nate's original design for the book cover. He only works in black and dark grays (like Batman).

If you have fan art to share, suggestions on how John can beat this curse, or historical figures you'd like to see, feel free to share! You can reach me at farts@derelictbooks.com.

About the Author

~~John Pahrsink~~ Michael J Adams is a grown man (at least on the outside) who loves writing and still finds fart humor funny. He lives with his wife and two children in the suburbs of Chicago.

In what little spare time he has, Michael enjoys video games and doing crafts with his kids.

You can follow Michael via these outlets:
Website: www.derelictbooks.com
Facebook: @DerelictBooks
Instagram: @MJAAuthor
Stay up to date by joining his newsletter: